SH

AT THE

MOON

SHOOT
AT THE
MOON

WILLIAM F. TEMPLE

With an Introduction by
MIKE ASHLEY

This edition published 2018 by
The British Library
96 Euston Road
London NW1 2DB

Originally published in 1966 by Ronald Whiting & Wheaton Ltd.
Copyright © 2018 Estate of William F. Temple
Introduction copyright © 2018 Mike Ashley

Cataloguing in Publication Data
A catalogue record for this book is available from the British Library

ISBN 978 0 7123 5256 7

Frontispiece from *Astronomie populaire* by Camille Flammarion, Paris, 1880.

Typeset by Tetragon, London
Printed and bound by CPI Group (UK) Ltd, Croydon CR0 4YY

SHOOT
AT THE
MOON

INTRODUCTION

William F. Temple hoped that *Shoot at the Moon* would be the novel to revive his career. He was in his mid-fifties and was finding that the growing shift in British science fiction towards the New Wave, with writers like J. G. Ballard, Michael Moorcock and Brian W. Aldiss, was skewing the market for his more traditional form of sf.

During the 1950s he had been one of Britain's top sf writers and he was voted Author of the Year in 1957 by readers of *Nebula SF* magazine. Following his success with *Four-Sided Triangle* in the early 1950s, Temple took the risk of becoming a full-time writer, always a challenge at a time when the science-fiction markets were low-paying both in Britain and the United States. Although he sold regularly to magazines in both countries, finding openings for novels proved difficult. He was able to sell a series of books for younger readers featuring Martin Magnus, Special Investigator of the Scientific Bureau, which saw three titles in the mid-fifties. He also compiled *The True Book About Space Travel* (1954) and wrote a series of stories for the short-lived *Rocket* children's comic.

But these British markets were unreliable and with a wife and family to look after Temple had to find full-time work again in 1957. Ironically just at that time the markets opened again, though almost all in the United States. He reworked several earlier magazine stories into the novels *The Automated Goliath* (1962), *The Three Suns of Amara* (1962) and *Battle on Venus* (1963).

His heart, though, was in working on something new and different and *Shoot at the Moon* was the first that readers saw of Temple's change of direction. It still shows his ability to build interesting characters, and his irrepressible sense of humour, often more sardonic than hilarious. The lead character and first-person narrator could easily be Temple himself. It betrays his latter-day world-weary grumpiness at how the world is falling apart because of the media and the rise of consumerism. Most significantly, though, it goes against the grain in considering how the first British moon-landing would be organized. It was a deliberate parody. Rather than bring together a well-trained and well-meshed team, Temple creates an idiosyncratic crew of deceitful, manipulative, uncaring and uncooperative individuals who do their best to thwart the actions of others. It should be no surprise that once these people are let loose on Britain's first moon trip, just about everything that could go wrong will go wrong – but not in the way you might expect.

Once on the moon there are two unexplained deaths and the novel shifts from being one of lunar exploration to a murder mystery in which everyone is a likely suspect. Yet the conclusion of the novel will come as a satisfactory surprise.

Temple's American agent sold the novel to Simon & Schuster in 1965 and the publisher was delighted. There were plans for a big promotion and a film option was taken by ABC Pictures. Temple thought that at last his luck was changing.

However, a sarcastic review in the *New York Times* soured the publisher on the book. The promotion was revoked and, with a change of staff at ABC Pictures, the film option was not renewed. Temple's hopes were dashed. When his next novel, *The Fleshpots of Sansato*, was savagely edited by New English Library, Temple gave up.

Yet *Shoot at the Moon* was highly regarded within the sf community. There were several positive reviews. Hilary Bailey remarked that 'Temple's perception of character is impressive', whilst Judith Merril revealed that 'a few scenes on the Moon gave me genuine chills...'. The novel is really a blend of the traditional and the radical, and perhaps because of that has never sat easily within the field. Its approach to the Space Race is, of course, rather dated now, though it was an intentional parody, and we can still view it as an alternative history in which a group of oddballs discover that the Moon is not what it seems.

Disillusioned, Temple returned to full-time work and barely wrote again. He did toy with the idea for a novel on faith-healing, but when his UK agent told him there'd be no market, he dropped it. Temple died in July 1989 aged 75, his potential never fully realized. His work has been overlooked for several decades but the publication of this new edition, together with the reissuing of *Four-Sided Triangle*, should attract new readers to these unduly forgotten novels.

MIKE ASHLEY

Happily we all shoot at the moon
with ineffectual arrows; our hopes
are set on an inaccessible El Dorado.

ROBERT LOUIS STEVENSON
Virginibus Puerisque (El Dorado)

I

SOMEONE HAD PAINTED ACROSS THE SLIDING DOORS, IN LETters big as saucers and red as arterial blood: KEEP OUT. And below that: NO ADMITANCE. The lettering was better than the painter's ideas about spelling or courtesy.

Both lapses irritated me.

All through the journey to this place I'd been getting ever more tetchy along with getting ever more scared. I was scared of what I knew lay waiting for me behind these doors. I was even more scared of my ignorance of it.

The security guards at the gate on the perimeter of this one-time airfield had checked me down to my teeth-fillings. Yet once I was over that hurdle no one cared even a small curse what I did. It appeared that the mere fact of being within the palisade guaranteed you were 'all right'. You and Caesar's wife were equally above suspicion, even if the pair of you were wearing parachute harness and consulting maps.

This was the only building labelled with warning notices. So that told me that it was the one I was looking for. The sign-painter might just as well have completed the job by adding: THIS BUILDING HOUSES THE TOP SECRET HARWELL ATOMIC PROPULSION UNIT.

I seized both handles of the doors. Earlier, I'd have imagined this simple act would cause an outbreak of alarums and excursions, peals of bells ringing, red lights flashing, armed motor-cyclists converging on me with shrieking sirens. But not now. Not after I had registered the evidences of general ineptitude around here.

I pulled the handles apart, the doors with them. 'KEEP' and 'NO' sped one way and 'OUT' and 'ADMITANCE' the other. Well, at least someone had kept the door runners well oiled.

And there it was, the HAPU, alone in the centre of the great concrete floor as though it had been laid there like an egg. A metal egg.

Not that it was an ovoid. Actually, it was a truncated cone twenty feet tall, dwindling upwards in diameter from around thirty-five feet to a bit under thirty. What I could see of it from here was smooth and seamless.

All framework had been removed from it. Apart from the fitting of it as a unit in the space-ship *Endeavour*, work on it was finished.

I walked over to look closely at the thing which had scared me and cost me sleepless nights. Now that I saw it in reality, it was so utterly featureless that my attention soon wandered from it. I gazed around the former hangar, but that was almost as bare.

There was a door in the far wall. From this distance it looked as small as the door to Alice's enchanted garden. I took a pace towards it. Almost as though I had trodden on a hidden spring, the door opened.

The man in the white laboratory coat who came through looked small, too, at first. As he walked deliberately towards me, he seemed to grow like a magic beanstalk. When he stopped, a couple of paces away, he was looking down at the top of my head. He was all of six and a half feet tall, and thin with it. I was – and still am – five feet five and a half inches, and not all that thin.

He had a beak of a nose, darkly notable eyebrows, darkly deep-set eyes. Dark hair receded from a near-islanded tuft that was formerly a widow's peak. His expression was dark, too. He put me in mind of some Latin-European actor playing Sherlock

Holmes, well made up but aware he was miscast and so feeling resentful.

He stared down at me, kept his hands at his sides like a footman, and said in a voice as thin as his body and as deliberate as his gait: 'You are...?'

I reached, rapidly, some conclusions. One was that I disliked him. His inquiry was unnecessary. He knew who I was. I was expected at this time, and the guard had phoned from the gate to report my arrival.

For some reason he wasn't overjoyed to see me. Also he regarded me as a waste of his time, someone not worth the bother of knowing because I had no power to pull any strings on his behalf. So I must be put in my place from the outset.

Hence the imperious, 'You are...?' with raised eyebrow.

I said, quietly, conspiratorially: 'I'm Professor Moriarty. Do you have any secret plans for sale? At the usual trade discount, of course.'

His other eyebrow went up to join its mate.

'Please. I do not understand. Your accent...'

I tried not to smile and spoil it. He had a Polish accent a yard thick.

He was, I guessed, Harwell's boy wonder (only twenty-nine, though he looked forty), originally from Cracow but now naturalized British. The HAPU was largely his brain-child.

My name is Franz Brunel. My parents came from Alsace-Lorraine, but I was born in London. There's cockney in my accent – intermittently.

I said: 'I'm Captain Brunel, as you're perfectly well aware. I'm here by appointment to meet Colonel Marley and have my duties explained. Also, to have this power unit explained, presumably by your goodself. You sent me a sheet of instructions, together with a letter – I couldn't decipher the signature.'

He ejaculated something. It sounded like a curse.

'I beg your pardon,' I said, coldly.

'My name is—' And he repeated the sound, deliberately.

I still didn't get it. For that matter, I never really did get it. It sounded like 'Zignawitsch', and in this chronicle, anyhow, Zignawitsch he will have to be.

Here and now, I may as well admit to a long-standing fault of character which has generated trouble enough in my life. I'm super-sensitive about courtesy. I can tolerate my own bad manners but not other people's. I suffered much from snubs when young, and – worse – had to watch my father suffer them.

The high-handed are my natural enemies in life.

Early poverty and insecurity bred in me a sense of social inferiority. From this grew an outsize chip on my shoulder. Whistler could paint, in his time. I never could. Whistler had a mother. I never knew mine. But I could always match Whistler in the gentle art of making enemies.

A bad trait, this, in a space-pilot. If he can't control it he should be disqualified. It doesn't matter on the transatlantic rocket ferry run. That trip doesn't last an hour and the pilot sits for'ard in his little cabin – alone. But space-ship trips are a deal longer and there's seldom any segregation.

When the ships start going regularly beyond the moon on the months' long trips to the planets – and those days have become much nearer because of the events in this narrative – social misfits of my sort may find it hard to get a job on them. A crew must be able to hit it off. As Mountbatten said long ago: 'A happy ship is an efficient ship.' The converse is also true.

So Zignawitsch's attitude riled me. I suspected he was responsible for the curt, misspelt notice on the hangar doors. Still, these were pinpricks. The tap-root of my antipathy lay much deeper. He was responsible for the HAPU and what it might do to me.

I flicked the smooth side of the thing and asked: 'Can you show me the works?'

Zignawitsch said, 'In an atomic reactor there is not much "works". There are but a few sliding parts, and if they are—'

He fumbled for a word.

'Slid!' I offered.

'Moved,' he said, frowning. 'If they are moved, the reactor starts—'

He seemed weak on English verbs and once more sought the *mot juste.*

'Reacting?'

Again he rejected my help, plainly resenting it. 'The reactor starts working, and then it is fatal to be exposed to the radiations.'

'I wasn't exactly planning to put my head inside the oven,' I said. 'I assumed the thing might be opened by remote control and observed, if necessary, by TV. I gather that's the normal drill. But then, of course, I'm not a technical type. All I know is what I read in the papers. I could be wrong or – even worse – out of date.'

He stiffened himself so rigorously against the barbs that I feared he'd get cramp.

Bleak as an east wind, he said, 'The HAPU is sealed tight. It can be opened only on these premises and then only by qualified inspectors. And that is not for what I am employed. The mechanism is secret. Also it is a precision job. An amateur attempt at repair might damage it beyond repair.'

I had one of those 'I-have-been-here-before' feelings. Then suddenly, through a dusty corridor of memory, I saw a clear and bright picture of myself as a kid asking the friendly chauffeur of my father's snooty employer if he would show me the engine of his car.

'Sorry, Franz,' he said. 'But it's a Rolls, you see. All Rolls' bonnets are sealed tight and should be opened only by the proper inspectors. The engines are so beautifully made that the makers don't want any old people tampering with them.'

I returned to the present, and found myself scowling, which wasn't unusual.

'What in fact you're telling me is that if I damage this unit while landing the *Endeavour* on the moon, I'm not to attempt any running repairs but just tuck it under my arm and bring it back here for one of your inspectors to have a look-see?'

'Something like that,' said Zignawitsch, without humour.

'Very well, then, let me have a chat with an inspector.'

'There would be no point, Captain Brunel. He would not be allowed to tell you any more about the Harwell Atomic Propulsion Unit than is contained in that instruction sheet I sent you.'

I retrieved the sheet from an inner pocket.

I read aloud: '"To start the reaction, press once the button marked *Start*. Reaction ceases when the adjacent button marked *Stop* is pressed once. The damping effect is regulated automatically by the Earth radar altimeter and the lunar radar altimeter respectively."'

I screwed up the sheet and threw it on the floor.

'That,' I said, 'is followed by two paragraphs of similar pointless guff. It adds up to this: apart from starting and stopping the ship, a pilot will be so much dead weight.'

The Harwell Prodigy looked past my left ear and said nothing.

'All right, we'll allow he can use his skill on occasion. At least it's up to him to judge the right moments to press the buttons. That almost makes his trip worth while.'

Zignawitsch continued to look past me. A spasm of malice twisted the corner of his mouth.

He said: 'It does not matter whether he judges or misjudges. Nor whether he presses the buttons or not. If they are not pressed within a second of the right moment, a relay... er...'

He reviewed his vocabulary, his lips moving slightly.

'Clicks,' he said, suddenly. 'A relay clicks over and switches the controls from manual to automatic. We cannot afford to take any chance. This unit is our only prototype and it cost the Earth.'

The moment of truth, which I had feared all along, had come.

In all my experience of it, I've never liked the feeling of 'free fall'. Especially the first moment of it, when the rocket motors are switched off, the feeling of weight at once departs, and there's nothing to get a purchase on.

You can't help feeling that something's gone terribly wrong, and the ship is falling and you with it. For me that first moment is of panic, always – panic because of insecurity.

But that moment passes. As this one passed. I became suddenly cool and very much aware, the way most space-pilots do when danger comes. Those who lose their nerve at such times are likely soon to lose their lives also.

Still, this was no mere split rocket tube or an unexpected, uncharted meteor stream. The danger I smelt was not of losing my life but of losing my livelihood.

And yet – it *was* my life. For life to me meant having, besides good money, personal significance. To be my own boss, on my little planet-ship in space, to explore, to have adventures, to defy airless death.

All ever the world now automation was pensioning off people of my age. Some were being educated for leisure. Many were content to laze, anyway, with hands folded across their widening waists. The more energetic got their kicks from sport.

The more sedate stuck to the gaming tables. The earnest studied modern languages and/or travelled.

For my own type there were few opportunities left for physical exploration on Earth – except in amatory directions. The latter held little appeal for me and it was getting a bit late to consider them now. I never wanted any entanglements that could tie me down to Earth. I had never known real happiness on Earth.

I had no need to sit there and cry for the moon – I had long ago set out to get the moon. When, in time, I got it, there would still be no end to the adventure. There would remain a whole group of new worlds to conquer within the solar system.

Man was really beginning to move along the third dimension, and I was in the vanguard. So I felt significant. Until now.

I stared hard at Zignawitsch. He still refused to meet my eyes. I thought: 'Maybe, after all, it isn't quite so cut and dried as you boffins like to pretend.'

If he'd been putting up a bluff, I decided to call it.

Aloud, I said: 'I shan't tamper with your box of tricks. Obviously, it's so capable of looking after itself that it can find its own way to the moon. Let it, then. I'm clearly redundant. Therefore, I'll resign from the Service.'

'*Resign?*' echoed a voice with a crack of authority about it which set my hackles up right away. '*Resign?* You can't resign from the Space Service. You're under contract, my man, as well you know.'

Yes, I knew. I was under contract for two more years. My fear was that the contract wouldn't be renewed. I had cropped my hair but the grey filaments still glinted. I limbered up every morning but my reflexes were losing their former snap.

And these days I stood uneasily in the shadow of this latest offspring of automation, the robot space-pilot.

I turned. Through the still parted hangar doors three men had come and were approaching, one behind the other. When they halted they were still more or less in line, consciously or not in order of size – and maybe of importance.

The foremost was nearly as tall as Zignawitsch but broad in proportion: a massive man. He had the shoulders of a champion weight-lifter. He was grinning, with a down-turned mouth, like Punch... or a shark. And yet he was frowning, too. The effect was formidable.

I'd seen that face somewhere before, probably on TV. I wished it were on TV now, so that I could switch it off.

I'd have said he was sixty years old and had been overbearing for most of them. I disliked him on sight.

That was Colonel Marley.

On the other hand, I liked the look of the young man standing behind him. He was tallish, too, and nicely built. He was one of those men you can tell are Scots right away by their eyes. Not merely because their eyes are bright blue and their eyebrows so light as to be almost colourless. The clue is something about the shape of the upper eyelid. It makes their eyes look quizzical and humorous, even when these men have no sense of humour at all and are ninety per cent proof Calvinists.

It's easy to be mistaken about them, and I certainly made a mistake about this specimen.

But Doctor Thomson had a sense of humour – of a kind.

Behind him was a small dried-up chap, mild-eyed and melancholy as a lotos-eater. His skin was the colour of milky coffee, cracked, large-pored, and most unhealthy-looking. I gave him a year to live and was wrong again.

He was hunched up as though he were afraid of taking up too much room in this place which was as roomy as a gasometer. His bluish lips were gummed together as though they hadn't parted in days. Obviously, he wasn't going to speak unless spoken to, and maybe not even then.

He was either an old young man or a young old man. I couldn't guess at his age, but one thing was certain: Melancholy had marked him for her own.

That was Pettigue.

The authoritative voice cracked again like a whip. It came from the big plug-ugly in the forefront, where it was his nature to be.

'Did you hear what I said, my man?'

'Yes,' I said, slowly. 'There was distortion from blasting but, yes, I heard. Don't "my man" me. I'm just not your man.'

Zignawitsch's eyebrows shot up. He was shocked.

Grinning like a fiend, the big fellow asked: 'You're Captain Franz Brunel?'

'You're right this time.'

'Then, like it or not, you *are* my man. I'm Colonel Marley.'

I'd guessed that. Nevertheless, the confirmation made me feel almost as melancholy as Pettigue looked. It was never my luck to have dealings with anyone I could naturally rub along with. Marley was in charge of this project. Marley was my master. It had to be someone I hated on sight.

'I see,' I said.

The grin remained there like the Cheshire Cat's but the rest of the face looked even more unpleasant than before.

'You see what?' asked Marley, dropping his voice to what he hoped was an impressive and dangerous quietness.

'I see that you're Colonel Marley.'

The grin suffered a slow death. Marley said, harshly: 'Do you never address your superior officers in the Space Service as "sir"?'

'Always. But you're not my superior officer in the Space Service. You're not in the Space Service at all. You're Army, and retired at that. I'm under your orders, admittedly. I'll even obey them. But I'm not bound to salute you. Heel-clicking is out. I'll face a court martial first.'

'Silence!' he roared. 'Stand to attention!'

I sighed. 'Go to hell,' I said, tiredly. 'Take the shortest route.'

Obviously, this defiance of authority was painful for Zignawitsch to witness. He stared at the roof and pretended none of us was there.

Red-faced, wordless, Marley tried to slay me on the spot with a Gorgon look. I remained impervious. Abruptly he turned his back to me and his glare on the HAPU. It wouldn't melt either.

That left Thomson as the only person apparently aware of my existence. He regarded me even more quizzically, and held out his hand.

'I'm Thomson, the medico on this trip.'

I nodded, and shook his hand.

He had an Edinburgh burr I shan't attempt to render. It was noticeable when he attempted to introduce the diminutive zombie behind him.

'This is Pettigue. He's a government prospector, geologist, metallurgist, qualified surveyor, and all-round explorer. He's been all over the world. Now, like us, he's been assigned to the next world.'

It would be an exaggeration to say that Pettigue came alive. But his eyes – pale as boiled onions – slowly turned in my direction and seemed attracted by the glitter of my waist-belt buckle. Without raising them, he deposited a small brown monkey-claw of a hand in mine and left it there. I held it for a moment, wondering whether I was expected to warm it into life, and then gave it back to him. He let it fall disinterestedly to his side. He seemed to regard it as a mere appendage.

His lower jaw moved. I thought he was about to speak, but I expected too much. He was merely changing the position of a wad of chewing gum. But he didn't want to work on it. His face became quiescent again. I wondered why he troubled to carry the gum around at all.

Thomson shrugged and smiled at me. Plainly he had no time for Pettigue, and I didn't feel inclined to spare much, either.

Zignawitsch was still staring at the ceiling, Marley at the HAPU, and Pettigue was back to watching nothing.

I remarked to Thomson: 'Do you have a pack of cards on you? We could play poker.'

Thomson shook his head, still smiling, and turned to the Harwell Prodigy. 'You must be Dr Zignawitsch.'

Zignawitsch brought his gaze down, applied it to empty space before him, and – to shame me – stood to attention without being told to.

Marley turned to look on him with approval. 'Yes, this is Zignawitsch. He's a genius.'

Zignawitsch's chest expanded more, as though the Colonel were pinning a medal to it. This was one of his big moments.

Marley said confidentially to Thomson: 'My friend Howard, the Minister of Supply, expects big things of Dr Zignawitsch. He thinks he'll be running Harwell before he's forty.'

Zignawitsch's eyebrows began to twitch with emotion.

Thomson said: 'Yes, I'd heard the HAPU is largely your baby, Doctor. Could you tell us what makes it tick?'

Zignawitsch, who'd behaved to me like a human clam, became eager to open up his small heart to these bigger bugs. For them he trotted out his top secret files, verbally.

In brief, the HAPU solved the problems which hitherto had barred the way to the full-scale atomic rocket-ship. The problem of rapid heat transference to the propellant (hydrogen in this case) had been met by a new method of direct contact with the fissioning element.

The old problem of the near impossible weight of shielding material needed to protect crews from atomic radiation had also been overcome. All particles flying in the direction of the living quarters of the ship were (after they had heated the hydrogen) caught by a deflector and cast harmlessly into space.

This deflector wasn't just a curved electrode, like that in a cyclotron which bends back the paths of high-speed particles. It was a pattern of magnetic fields which performed the same deflecting duty far more effectively.

So far as I was concerned, Zignawitsch need never have opened his files on this magnetic field pattern. I understood about one word in six of its principles. He could have been talking in Polish.

I doubt if the others were any wiser, either, but one could never tell about Pettigue. He still looked as though rigor mortis was about to set in.

During the discourse, Marley's grin slowly returned. He assumed a proprietorial interest in Zignawitsch. At the end, he announced: 'You see, gentlemen, Harwell's taken care of everything.'

He markedly avoided my eyes when he said 'gentlemen'.

Thomson, who was markedly included, said: 'Mightn't there be a wee spot of trouble after the take-off? Among the local inhabitants, I mean. The ship will squirt the atmosphere full of radio-activated hydrogen, which wouldn't be exactly healthy for them.'

Zignawitsch answered politely: 'The ship will be – er – launched from a – um – disinhabited island in the Pacific Ocean. It will cause no more harm than an atomic bomb exploded under test conditions.'

Dr Thomson shrugged.

'All the same,' continued Zignawitsch, registering a hint of pain, 'the government is not prepared to take the smallest risk. They have – er – insisted that the HAPU is not to be brought into action until the height of one hundred miles is reached, where atmosphere is negligible.'

Marley caught the note of protest. 'The P.M. insisted on that, not I,' he said, quickly.

I stared at Zignawitsch and asked: 'And how do you propose to get the *Endeavour* up to that height of one hundred miles – fire it from a catapult?'

Zignawitsch ignored me.

'How?' Thomson pursued.

'By a chemical – er—' fumbled Zignawitsch, looking sullen.

'Booster rocket,' I supplied, and saw that I was right. 'So a human pilot *is* necessary, after all.'

'Not in my opinion,' said Zignawitsch, glacially. 'The take-off could be radio-controlled from the ground – it would be easy. The dropping of the booster could be automatic. The HAPU is automatic in any case.'

'You're straying from your beat, son,' I said. 'You'd do better to stick to your atomic physics. If ground control is the best way, why hasn't it been used on all the chemical ships so far? Don't bother to refuse to answer – I'll tell you. It's because no instruments you back-room boys have cooked up yet have been half as reliable as these.'

I held out my hands.

I went on: 'No servo-motors can do what these can do – the hands of an experienced space-pilot. These finger-tips can *feel*. When they're on the controls, those controls become extensions of my nerves. Oh, I've had it happen scores of times, testing controls which your meters say are okay – but my nerves tell me are not. My reflexes are one hundred per cent reliable. Your automatic gadgets, at a generous estimate, rate no more than ninety-seven per cent accuracy. You and the Colonel here have forgotten something: in his youth, the Prime Minister was a jet-plane test pilot.'

'Well hit, sir,' said Dr Thomson.

Zignawitsch seemed to have run out of words, even the wrong ones.

Marley said, expressionlessly: 'I side with Zignawitsch about this. I make no secret of it – I said as much to the P.M. The *Endeavour* will make space-pilots obsolete. The very first flight will show that that conclusion can't be avoided. But we must indulge the P.M. He's a little sentimental – perhaps all great men are. I must confess that I myself regret the human factor being supplanted by electronic machines. But we must accept it. It's the trend of this civilization.'

'And so I'm to ride as a sort of mascot,' I said, bitterly.

'You're to ride because the Prime Minister has so ordered it,' snapped Marley. 'The nature of your duties I shall explain to you tomorrow. Be at my house at three in the afternoon – the address is twenty-three, Elm Gardens, Chelsea. Make sure you're on time, Brunel.'

'*Captain* Brunel,' I emphasized.

He presented me with his back view again. It was no thing of beauty, but I preferred it to the frontal aspect. He began talking to Thomson in little more than a whisper. This palaver was finished as far as I was concerned.

I walked over to the hangar doors. Zignawitsch followed leisurely, one pace to every two of my short legs. He was keen to see me off the premises.

At the doors, I glanced back. My three prospective fellow-travellers to the moon were still grouped under the sawn-off cone of the HAPU.

Marley. Thomson. Pettigue.

I wondered how we should fare together. I anticipated a certain amount of unpleasantness. But at that moment I certainly had no premonition that two of them would never come back from the moon alive.

Or dead.

A moment later, I was outside the doors, and 'NO ADMITANCE' came together with a bang, as if it really meant it. By now I suspected that it did.

II

ELM GARDENS WAS NEAR SLOANE SQUARE. IT LOOKED AS though a playful giant had set a hand at either end of the thoroughfare and compressed it, shortening it and squashing the terraced houses until they became tall and thin.

I peeped through the iron railings into the basement of Twenty-three. There were a couple of uniformed maids playing cards at a table, for all the world as though it were still the golden age of Queen Victoria. Servants, I'd begun to think, belonged almost entirely to the B.A. era: Before Automation.

I rang. Half a minute later, one of the maids opened the door, breathless and a little resentful.

'Sorry to interrupt the game just when you were holding all the trumps,' I said, 'but Colonel Marley is expecting me. I'm Captain Brunel.'

'The Colonel ain't back yet, sir.'

I glanced at my watch. Three o'clock, within seconds.

'Probably his watch is an hour slow. I find that common among people of his kind. Odd, but there you are.'

A door opened somewhere down the long hall and a Girton College voice called: 'If that's Captain Brunel, Teresa, send him along.'

'Very good, Miss Marley,' answered Teresa, and sent me along. These houses, I realized, were much larger than they seemed from without. It was quite a walk to the far end of the hall where the door stood ajar.

I tapped.

'Come right in, Captain,' said the cultured voice.

I stepped in and sank almost to my ankles in the Oxford blue fitted carpet.

I knew nothing about Marley's family. Was 'Miss Marley' his sister or his daughter? She had her back to me and was bending over a tape-player. All I saw was a pair of black jeans too amply filled. Miss Marley's posterior would have delighted Velasquez. In this day and age it would have been better concealed than revealed.

His sister, I decided.

She straightened up and turned, to soft music from the player.

My mistake. A man of sixty was unlikely to have a sister of under thirty – even though maybe only a couple of years under. This was Marley's daughter.

'I'm Lou. Daddy told me to expect you around this time. I'm to entertain you till he comes. He shouldn't be long – he's such a busy man, you know.'

I nodded, attempted to smile, and wished I could lose the misanthropic streak which seldom failed to make me dislike each new acquaintance on sight. I disapproved of fat females in their late twenties who still referred to their father as 'Daddy', prevalent though the habit might be in this upper social stratum.

A generous man would have said Miss Marley was merely plump. Right then I didn't feel like a generous man. She had shining black hair and shining black eyes. Her nose was straight and her chin might have looked good, too, if it weren't for the other one supporting it. At one time, probably, she had been really good-looking. But she'd let herself run to fat.

Maybe someone had told her black made you look slimmer. If so, she'd taken it to heart. She was wearing a black blouse, belt, and slippers, as well as the black jeans. *In toto,* they did nothing for her.

I suppose I looked her up and down too obviously.

'Do you know why I dress all in black?' she asked, suddenly.

'Because it doesn't show the dirt?'

'No.' She struck a mock tragic pose. 'Because I'm in mourning for my life.'

Masha's line from *The Seagull,* and the only one I could recall, for it occurs in the first few minutes, and I'd dozed off after that.

'Do you like Chekhov?' pursued Miss Marley.

'No.'

'I don't think you like *anybody* very much,' she remarked, shrewdly. 'Have a choc?'

She picked up one of three boxes lying around and proffered it.

'No, thanks.'

She scrutinized the contents, murmuring to herself: 'Lou – you're going to find it hard to entertain Captain Brunel.'

She selected the largest of the chocolates and popped it into her mouth. It was quite a firm mouth, I noticed.

'I'm sorry about that, Miss Marley.'

'Call me Lou,' she said, indistinctly: she'd picked a caramel.

'Is that the diminutive for Louise or Louisa?'

'Could be, but my name is Lou. There's no more to it. I'm the lady that's known as Lou.'

I looked blank.

'She's in *The Shooting of Dan McGrew,*' she explained.

'Yes, I know. All the same, I just don't get it.'

'It was *I* who got it,' she said, wryly. 'Daddy gave it to me.'

'But why—'

'You don't know Daddy very well, do you?' she cut in.

'Hardly at all.'

'You'll soon learn why,' she said, cryptically.

I was in no hurry, and knew as much as I cared to of Marley. I looked casually around the room. It was big. There were rows of open bookshelves, a monster TV set, and a couch almost hidden by a multitude of carelessly heaped cushions. I never saw so many cushions in one room. They made bright islands everywhere on the dark blue sea of the carpet. On one of them a fat, black cat was curled up asleep.

Also scattered around the floor were bowls of fruit and nuts and all kinds of candy.

The window opened on to the back yard, a tiny patio containing just enough space to stack the gardening implements that weren't needed.

'You don't like Lou's room, either, do you, Captain?'

'A bit too sybaritic for my taste.'

'Lou likes comfort.' She sat cross-legged beside the cat and began to stroke it gently. I sighed inwardly. A good education had been wasted on a plain case of arrested emotional development. I began to wish Marley would hurry up and come, say his piece, and I could escape.

Lou crooned to the cat, which didn't bother to prick up an ear. Languorous music from the *Mother Goose* Suite drifted from the tape-player. I shuffled impatiently. There were no hard chairs, nothing I could sit on without some loss of dignity – the massed eiderdown of the couch ensemble would, I felt, suck me into it like quicksands.

I eyed the array of confectionery. 'Throwing a children's party?'

'I beg your pardon?'

I gestured. 'All that sweet stuff.'

'Lou likes candy. Don't you, Captain?'

'Not much.'

She whispered to the cat: 'The Captain doesn't like candy, Mack. Do you think he likes cats? No, of course he doesn't. He doesn't like anybody or anything. He doesn't even like Lou.'

Exasperation comes easily to me, and it came then.

I snapped: 'Even Lou doesn't like Lou.'

She looked up sharply and her black eyes glinted. 'What makes you say that, Captain Brunel?'

'People who habitually refer to themselves in the third person are trying to stand apart from themselves, because they don't like themselves very much.'

Her gaze dropped. She scratched behind one of the cat's unresponsive ears. 'Hey, Mack, we've got to watch out. This fellow's as sharp as your claws. And he says what he thinks, too. Daddy won't like that, will he?'

The ear pricked up suddenly.

'Yes, that's Daddy,' Lou murmured. 'No more sleep for you now, Mack.'

I hadn't heard the front door open, but in a moment I felt as well as heard the heavy footfalls coming along the hall. The door was flung open and Marley, all beef, bounce, and shark's grin, made a stage entrance. The room seemed to fill at once with his cheap, overpowering personality.

Mack made an equally sudden exit, passing Marley at a rapid trot with his tail in the air.

'Daddy!' Buxom Lou hurled herself at her massive father, hugged him and kissed him. He responded with enthusiasm. All rather distasteful.

When it was over, Marley asked her, as though I was all of a hundred miles away: 'And what do you think of our little Captain?'

'Well, I'll say this: he knows his own mind. But I'd hate to say it was worth knowing.'

'You don't like him either, then?'

'That's beside the point, Daddy. It's better to have a Captain who knows his own mind than a ditherer always in two minds.'

'So long as his mind doesn't conflict with mine,' said Marley, and looked at me grimly over her shoulder.

'I'm sure we'll get along fine,' I said. 'Sure as today's Tuesday.'

'It's Wednesday,' he said, after a pause.

I shrugged.

Lou laughed. In contrast to the college voice, which inevitably struck me as affected although I was aware it was unconsciously acquired, her laugh was easy, deep, natural. Most surprising of all, sexy – why should I think that, who'd never associated sex and laughter before?

'Watch your step, Daddy. He bites.'

'H'm.' Marley regarded me thoughtfully. 'Like a drink?'

'I always did.'

'The bar's upstairs,' he said, abruptly. 'This way.'

He turned and strode out. As he turned, I noticed for the first time a long, thin scar across the right side of his neck. It was as straight as a sword cut. It had long since healed, but when it happened the vultures must have had high hopes. Marley, surely, was too full of life and conceit ever to attempt suicide? I'd never read of any homicidal attack on him, but I could have missed it. Out in space, one gets out of contact with the workaday world of murder, rape, robbery, and brutality. Maybe that was why I elected to go out in space…

Just another car smash, I told myself, and followed him.

I ignored a murmur behind me: 'Shocking manners!' The Marleys, father and daughter, had no call to protest about manners.

I met Mack again making a hasty exit, this time from the barroom door and with all four feet off the ground. Marley had literally kicked him out.

Mack was a stoic and made no sound. He fled down the stairs. Marley's voice boomed after him: 'Lou, if I catch Carmack in the "Pack Train" again he'll become meat for the undertaker. I won't have that stink in my bar.'

Carmack in the 'Pack Train'? I was puzzled, not least by the feeling I ought to know what the references meant. As soon as I entered the bar, I did know.

The bar itself ran the full length of a pretty long room. There was sawdust on the bare-boarded floor and battered spittoons stood in every corner, save one, where a Malemute dog squatted on its haunches. It was motionless, and at a second glance I saw it was expertly stuffed.

Moose-heads stared down glassily from the walls. Strewn between them were scores of framed, faded photographs.

A board, crumbling dustily at the edges, certainly old enough to be an original, hung over the bar. On it, dirty, flaking white paint proclaimed: THE PACK TRAIN INN.

Marley was already behind the bar, setting out three glasses. He sloshed whisky into them: there seemed no alternative drink.

I walked over. 'Quite an atmosphere,' I commented. 'Guess the Inn did look pretty much like this in the days when Soapy Sam was boss of Skagway.'

Marley glanced up, surprised.

'So you know something—' he began, then stared past me with

that angry maniacal grin. I looked around. Lou had just come in with an apprehensive-looking Mack clasped in her arms.

'Lou,' said Marley, quietly and ferociously, 'you heard what I said. Bring Carmack in here and I'll break his neck.'

Lou stopped. 'If he goes, Lou goes.'

'Then get to hell out of here,' Marley rasped.

Lou stared at him insolently for a moment, and then – oh, Girton, Girton! – spat on the floor. She never troubled to aim for one of the brass pots. Then she and Mack took their leave. The heavy door slammed, and the moose-heads shivered slightly.

'That damned cat!' growled Marley, and I wondered which of them he was referring to. He put away a glass of neat whisky with one steady swallow. 'I should never have given it to her. She already thinks more of it than she does of me.'

'Carmack? Did you name it after that prospector who – along with a couple of Indians – first struck gold in the Klondike?'

'Yes,' he said, surprised again. 'You seem to know your way around the Klondike Territory, Brunel.'

'It had a certain glamour for me at one time.'

'It has for me still. Know what, Brunel? If I could have picked a time in which to live, above all I'd have chosen to be a young man back in '98.'

'I'll take the present. It's even more stirring. Men are setting out to prospect whole new worlds.'

'But not for gold.'

'Gold is where you find it. Think of the new knowledge—'

'Knowledge!' Marley spat, right on target with a spittoon. He must have spent a deal of time practising. I had a momentary vision of Lou as a child in here, watching, imitating. This was the room where you were permitted to spit.

'I don't go for that "Man's Unconquerable Mind" guff,' said Marley. 'There are men who think, and men who do things without needing to think. Knowledge is something you learn with your nerves, not your brain. When the occasion comes, you should know what to do – instinctively.'

He reached for Lou's glass.

'Lou thinks too much,' he added, and began to drink.

Myself, I would have opined that Lou's thoughts seldom rose above food and creature comforts, but the opinion was scarce worth expressing. Instead, I secured my own glass, and with it safely in hand, wandered around inspecting the photo gallery.

None was labelled but I identified many of them. The Northern Saloon, in Front Street, Nome. The Sawtooth Mountains. The three-storey Golden Gate Hotel. A view of the White Pass. Klondike Kate. Tex Rickard. Jack London. Robert W. Service. Rex Beach. A six-horse stage. A homemade scow shooting some rapids. Dawson City.

And a big one of Chilkoot Pass itself. I studied it, then started as Marley spoke directly behind me: 'Imagine carrying a ton of food and equipment over that. Up an ice-slope of thirty-five degrees.'

'Tough. Where's this place? I don't recognize it.'

'That's Dead Horse Gulch. Three thousand pack horses died there trying to get through the mountains.'

He wanted to show me everything. It took time and several more drinks. But at the end of it he was almost amiable, almost human. Maybe it was the drink. More likely, the satisfaction of talking about what was dear to his heart to someone not entirely ignorant of the subject.

Everyone's got a hobby and at least the vestiges of an adolescent fantasy life. Marley's particular fad was no odder than some

I'd run across. If he got a kick from playing this game that he was a pan-handler plugging along the old Dyea Trail, seeking the big bonanza, then let him. It could do no harm.

What I didn't realize then was that it was no game. And it could do harm, all right.

He said: 'You've gathered by now, Brunel, that adventure is life to me. That's why I jumped at this moon project. We can't all be Carmacks, the first in the field. But there was plenty left for those who followed Carmack – the real pickings, as it turned out. Alaska was big. The moon's a damn sight bigger. There's plenty left there for us. And our ship is way out in front of anything that's been built up till now.'

'So I've gathered. But there's been so much hush-hush I don't even know what the *Endeavour* looks like.'

'I'll show you. Down in the library.'

I was back to following at his heels.

The library had one occupant: Lou. She was filling most of a big saddle-bag easy chair, her feet up on a walnut writing-desk. The inevitable box of candy lay on the chair-arm. She was studying a book and chewing.

'What are you doing here?' asked Marley, towering above her.

She looked up with malice in her black eyes.

'Brushing up on toxicology: it might come in useful sometime.'

He stared at her coldly. 'It might, at that.'

He turned his attention to a wall safe. While he juggled with the combination lock, I glanced along the bookshelves. There was a whole section on exploration, particularly of the Far North. That I had expected to find, likewise the rows of military textbooks and memoirs, and a library in itself covering every aspect of politics.

But the shelves of scientific textbooks were a surprise. The main line was clearly biochemistry, but the general range was wide, touching on almost everything alphabetically from astronomy to zoology. Moreover, so far as my knowledge went, they were mostly works by leading specialists. No easy popularization here, but heavy going.

I rubbed my nose thoughtfully, but didn't solve the puzzle.

Marley came lumbering away from the safe carrying an envelope as wide as himself and as thick as my wrist. He slammed it on the desk, swept Lou's feet aside as though they were rubbish (she swore at him but went on reading) and extricated wads of engineering drawings.

I saw at a glance that the *Endeavour* was something quite different from the ship of my imagination. Not that I'd employed much imagination on it. I like streamlined elegance, and the conventional atmosphere-cleaving torpedo shape had always satisfied me aesthetically. I'd taken it for granted that the *Endeavour* would be of that design and merely bigger and better.

Instead… I saw something like an American doughnut with an inverted ice-cream cone wedged halfway through the hole in the middle. And, literally the crowning absurdity, on the point of the cone was perched an anything but atmosphere-cleaving little blob, like a fault in a poor casting.

I prodded it between annoyance and incredulity.

'What's the hell's that?'

'That,' said Marley, 'is the Captain's cabin. Your throne on high, Brunel. A little world of your own, which even I can't enter without your permission. There's balm for your ego.'

'Bounded in a nut-shell, counting himself king of infinite space,' murmured Lou, without looking up.

'Believe me, I'll appreciate the privacy,' I said. 'But what's the idea – am I to be quarantined? That blob looks to me like the ball on the top of the dome of St Paul's Cathedral, with one difference: it doesn't seem to belong to the rest of the structure.'

'In a sense, it doesn't,' said Marley. 'It's disengaged, like the free-wheel of a bicycle. It remains stationary, while the rest of the ship spins around its own axis. That big tubular ring, you see, contains the general living quarters. It's fixed on to the central cone, which contains the HAPU at its core. As the ring rotates, the angular momentum throws the occupants outward. They're pressed against the outer rim, the further wall of the tube from the centre. "Outward" is "downward" to them, in space. They'll walk on that wall as though it were the floor, and of course it'll seem just like a floor to them. They'll be under artificial gravity.'

I regarded him silently for a moment. He looked pleased with himself. Doubtless he was. He was lecturing as though he'd been acquainted with the science of space travel since its infancy. Yet I suspected that a couple of years ago he didn't even know why a rocket could propel itself through airless space. Maybe he still didn't know.

But he was a professional politician with long experience as a minister. He'd learned the trick of absorbing a handful of salient technical facts about Fisheries, Town-planning, Internal Economics, or whatever fresh world he was appointed to boss, and trotting them out with the assurance of a born master of the subject.

'Angular momentum' and all. He must have a mind like a tape-recorder.

I said: 'Artificial gravity is an old idea, though it's never actually been tried out in this way.'

'How could it be, Brunel, with the torpedo shape which gives it no scope? And while we were stuck with chemical fuels, we could never break away from the torpedo shape. Nor escape the problem of keeping the payload to a tight minimum. Even the pilots have had to keep their weight down. If you were anything like as big as I am, you would never have stood a chance of becoming a spaceman. In your day, pilots had to be built like jockeys.'

All true enough. I hated being undersized, but there was that point in its favour. Was I, then, lucky to be a little man? Maybe if I'd been of average height I should have been content to live an average life, and not be driven to seek compensation in the stature of a space hero.

All the same, any reference to my size made me bristle. I bristled. 'What d'you mean – in my day? I'm still in work.'

'Watch that blood-pressure, grandpa,' yawned Lou, shutting her book. But before she shut her mouth also she slipped another sweet into it.

'Yes, you're still in work – just about,' Marley grinned. 'Perhaps you'd better make the most of it, Brunel, for it may well be your last job. Like it or not, the robots are coming.'

Bullies have a way of smelling out one's would-be secret fears and sadistically harping on them. My dislike for Marley came boiling up again in the form of real hatred, but I screwed down the safety valve on it. He would get no more fun from that phobia at my expense.

I kept my face hard and said: 'The robots have already come. You can see them sitting in rows in the House of Commons.'

Annoyingly, he chuckled. 'I never claimed it took a brain to become a politician. In fact, it's almost as bad a handicap as a conscience. All you need is pig-headed obstinacy. You set a target, you reach it. Our current target is the moon. Let's return our attention to it. You are here to be made to grasp certain points about the ship you are to pilot…'

He went over the plans methodically for some minutes, explaining various aspects of the *Endeavour*. My attention wavered between his and my thoughts. I welcomed the prospect of artificial gravity. Some pilots I knew revelled in the three-dimensional skin-diving character of free fall. But I never liked it. The pumps never satisfactorily cleared the air of the millions of particles of dust and dirt which floated from the ship's interstices directly gravity's grip on them was relaxed. You had to watch your instruments through a faint haze.

That irritated me: I like to see things hard, sharp, and clear.

Again, other pilots were untroubled by eating and drinking under non-grav. But in space I suffered from chronic indigestion. No disgrace: Lord Nelson always suffered from sea-sickness aboard ship. I reckoned we were both highly-strung types.

Then there were the excretory processes… Artificial gravity would be a real boon there.

Funny, though, I had accepted these necessary unpleasant-nesses from the start as part of the spaceman's lot. And I never let them bother me until Pete Sykes died. Pete and I were pals from the first day at college. I beat him to the first solo flight by twenty-four hours.

We became ferry pilots serving the newly built space-station. Then one day his retro-rockets failed and he became marooned in orbit a thousand miles from the station. There were only three other ferry ships in operation, or supposed to be. Actually, they were grounded: the gremlins were running riot in all of them.

While I sweated blood with the technicians trying to get my ship operative, the Yanks made a brave but over-hasty attempt to reach Pete. A tank exploded and the two-man ship came down in confetti over the Florida Gulf.

I went after Pete at last in a ship with a dodgy parachute braking gear. I pulled alongside, airlock to airlock, maybe a half-hour after the last of his air reserve was used up. Suffocation was no easy way out, and Pete's appearance shocked every nerve in my system. This was such a crazy near-miss that I howled with anger and grief.

Sobbing and swearing I pulled him through into my ship. It was one of the most tragic things that had happened to me, but non-grav. had to play one of its silly tricks. God knows why, but Pete's body kept floating head down, feet up. That is, in relation to me, of course.

I expect we should have laughed like hell if he hadn't happened to be dead. I got him strapped up at last after a period of grim slapstick.

I remember looking out at the stars, after that. And thinking: What is thirty minutes measured on the astronomical scale?

Nothing. Nothing at all. Yet it was all the difference between life and death.

The stars seemed misty. I was seeing them literally through a mist of my own tears. The moisture had drifted away from my cheeks, resolving itself into a cloud of tiny globules each centred upon a point of dust.

That was when my dislike of free fall became absolute.

Probably I was the only pilot who loved space and at the same time wanted to feel his feet flat on the ground. I was becoming a pretty confused type.

'Flexibility in this connection is essential, so the entire length of it is articulated,' said Marley. He had been saying a lot of other things, too, but this one marked the point where I returned to full consciousness of his existence.

'Yes, I see that,' I said, brightly.

He was dealing with a large detailed plan of the Captain's cabin and the controls operable therefrom. He was engrossed in the drawing, so I rubbed my eyes, trying to make myself look as alert as I hoped I had sounded. My fingers came away wet. That picture from the past had been more vividly real than this room.

Watch it, Franz, I told myself. Sentimentality is an old man's luxury. So is mind-wandering. Hold on to your concentration, boy, or you really will be through as a pilot.

What the hell had Marley been saying? Never mind, I'd catch up with it in my own time.

Then I noticed Lou watching me.

Her eyes were as full of expression as a couple of black marbles. That wasn't because her mind was blank but because she was deliberately masking her thoughts.

I expected her to bleat: 'It's no use, Daddy, the Captain's not *with* it.'

But she remained silent, watching me.

'Lou thinks too much,' Marley had said.

What was she thinking now? I wished I'd been even half as prudent in covering up. To any percipient person I must have been quite a giveaway during these last few minutes.

And Lou was percipient, all right.

Again I'd lost the thread of Marley's discourse.

'Do you agree with that, Brunel?' he shot at me suddenly.

'Er... yes, of course.'

He stared at me glacially for a moment.

'Then the more fool you,' he said, abruptly, and began rolling up the plans.

That was a dropped brick I'd never be able to pick up, because I should never learn what it was.

Lou didn't laugh. Instead, she said: 'You still want me to come, Daddy?'

He swung his stare on to her. 'Naturally. You changed your mind now?'

'Yes. Lou will come.'

I thought they must be referring to a party or show.

'Good,' said her father. 'There'll be plenty of room for another Marley on the *Endeavour*. We'll make history *and* family history, girl.'

'I'm bringing Mack, too.' The challenge rang in her voice.

Marley became rigid. 'You're bloody not, you know.'

'I bloody am, you know.'

Marley made a wild swipe at her with the heavy roll of plans. I caught it on my forearm and stood between them.

I was feeling pretty mad myself, at both of them.

'Stop it!' I snapped. 'Who's gone crazy here? Are you seriously suggesting your daughter comes with us on my ship, Marley?'

His face was fire-red and his mouth was ugly.

'Suggesting, hell! She's coming if she wants to. Thomson and I have been pressing her to come right from the start. On *my* ship, Brunel, *my* ship.'

I took a deep breath and counted to five.

'The ship,' I said, quietly, 'belongs to the Commonwealth and the European Federation. So it's neither yours nor mine. It's inconceivable that the Government would tolerate the idea of pleasure trippers on a project of this importance. There would be an outcry from press and public. The Prime Minister—"

'The P.M. is in my pocket,' Marley interrupted, gratingly. 'So is half the press. As for the other half, it's mainly the popular press. They'll eat up the story. Feminine interest – that's their life-blood. They're hungry for heroines. They'll be on Lou's side. Young girl risks life in all-out attempt to reach the moon.'

'Young girl takes pet cat, from which she refuses to be parted,' said Lou. 'The British public goes overboard for pet animals. Why, it's a natural.'

'Carmack is *not* coming. That's final.' Marley glared.

'Black cats are lucky,' she said, calmly. 'Mack the Mascot of the Marleys. The British public laps up superstition—'

'*No!*' Marley thundered.

'Could be there are mice on the moon,' she said, reproachfully.

This pair would rip my sanity to shreds between them. I forgot to count, and shouted: 'Cats and women, they're both out! Or else *I* am.'

Marley ignored that. He'd dealt with that point before: I was under contract. He and Lou were silently trying to stare each other out. His hot, angry glare sought to beat down her cool, steady regard of him.

At length, it was Marley who broke off the duel. He looked at me, and said: 'A word of advice, Brunel. Don't ever marry. If you do, don't have children. If you do, don't have girls. If you do, drown them at birth.'

'For me, the problem isn't likely to arise.'

'H'm. That's just as well. You're a difficult person to get along with, Brunel, do you know that? I should feel really sorry for any family you acquired. You're impossibly impatient. You're always flying off the handle without pausing to learn the facts of the situation. You dismiss Lou out of hand – but what do you really know about her?'

His brassy nerve was incredible, but I was learning to take it as it came.

I said: 'Lou likes candy, cats, and getting her own way. She doesn't like me. I don't think she likes you – not all the time, anyhow. And she doesn't like herself. One can scarcely blame her. That's about all there seems to be. Of course, I may have missed some hidden depths, like a passion for vodka, rag dolls, and dominoes.'

Lou clapped her hands. 'Dominoes! Man, that's my game. Do you play, Captain? Will you give me a game?'

'How superficial can you get?' frowned Marley. 'D'you really believe my daughter is a moron? You think she got her degrees by family influence? You think her books were ghosted? You think Fellows of the Royal Society write only love-letters to her?'

There was a short pause while I reeled mentally from the punch, which affected my speech-centres.

'B-Books?'

'She's published eight, beside innumerable papers. Her *Organic Structures in Carbonaceous Meteorites* made ten languages – and four editions in this country alone. The *Times Science Review* said it was probably the most important scientific work of the year.'

'Hurrah for little Lou,' murmured the author.

My speech-centres refused to function at all now. Maybe they'd blown a fuse somewhere. I felt dumb in every way.

'Heavens, man,' snapped Marley, impatiently, waving a hand roughly in the direction of the science textbook shelves, 'you don't imagine *I* read that kind of stuff, do you? And certainly the damn cat doesn't.'

I remained dumb.

'You're embarrassing the Captain,' said Lou, rising. She caught up the box of candy and dropped it negligently in the waste-basket under the walnut desk. Bemused though I was, this struck me as a trifle odd, because the box was still half full. Perhaps she was the wasteful type.

Marley noted it, too. He raised an eyebrow. So it couldn't have been a characteristic act. Yet it meant something to him.

'That ends it?' he asked her.

'Yes.'

'It's been a long time, Lou.'

She shrugged.

'You're doing it for me?'

She shrugged again.

'For Tommy?'

'If it has to be for anyone, why not for me?' she said.

I didn't even try to make sense of it. Maybe later, when I could call my mind my own once more.

Lou held her hand out to me.

'Goodbye, Captain Brunel. See you on Peniwak.'

'On Peniwak,' I echoed, nodding, still unable to compose a simple sentence of my own.

She produced one final little surprise: her grip was something I might have expected from her old man but definitely not from his flabby-seeming daughter. The pain shot up my forearm.

She turned and went, quiet and unsmiling.

Marley watched her go. He was silent for a long minute afterwards. 'We might make out yet,' he said at last.

All these cryptic remarks weren't making it easy for me to find my way back to the sphere of communication. I passed.

'I'll ring you the day after tomorrow, Brunel. You'll have to attend training courses at Harwell, Salisbury, and maybe Woomera. Soon as I get the programme finalized, I'll give you your instructions.'

'Okay,' I managed. An inauspicious start, but nevertheless, a start.

By the time we'd reached the front door, my improvement was measurable. 'Goodbye, Colonel,' I said, faultlessly.

I went to a tavern in the King's Road and injected whisky until Franz was himself again. Then I rang Tod Reeves, an old pal, now editor of a Science Abstracts publication. I caught him at his office.

'Tod, this is Franz. I'm after information. Ever heard of the work of a certain Miss Lou Marley?'

'Marley? Is that L. A. Marley, the biochemist?'

'Possibly. Did L. A. Marley write a book about carbonaceous meteorites?'

'Yes, she did. It's a classic. She's pretty classy, all round, as I remember her. I met her once, at her publisher's office, some years ago... She quite threw me. The average bluestocking is left-on-the-shelf material, you know, homely and bitter about it. But the Marley girl was a real good-looker, a brunette with a figure like Gabrielle Gavin's. She set me dreaming for a time, until I learned she was already married.'

'Married?'

'Yes, married – to her work. A beautiful dish going to waste in the lab. So far as I gathered, to her love was merely a biochemical reaction. I concluded she was one of nature's little ironies: a fine male mind functioning in a fine female body. Striking, remarkable – but quite unattainable. Anyhow, what's your sudden interest in her?'

Confusion was trying to smother me again. I was no film-TV fan, but like most people I'd seen plenty of photos of Gabrielle Gavin. She was famed for her figure. And it was a sylph-like figure and had never been otherwise.

'I may have to work with her,' I said, carefully. 'Say, Tod, how far did you really know her?'

He laughed ruefully. 'I never got nearer to her than the width of her publisher's desk. I saw her only that once. The rest was wishful fantasy, hearsay gossip, and pure conjecture. About the only concrete facts I can give you is a list of her published works.'

'I see. Maybe you can answer another question. Where or what is Peniwak?'

'Spell it, old man.'

'I don't know how to. Peniwak. Doesn't it mean anything to you either?'

'Not a thing. I'll make a guess: the tenth planet.'

'Try your gazetteer. Peniwak – maybe with one "n", maybe with two.'

'Okay, Franz, hold on.'

A little later: 'You there, Franz? Peniwak is a small, isolated island in the Pacific.'

'I might have guessed it – the disinhabited island.'

'Don't you mean "uninhabited"? You sound to me as though you've been drinking, Franz.'

'Maybe that's because I've been drinking, pal.'

Tod chuckled. 'Well, all right, give my regards to the Marley woman if and when you meet up with her. She's a bit of a mystery in academic circles these days. Nobody seems to know whether she's still working or not. She hasn't published anything in years. People are wondering what happened to her.'

'I'm one of them,' I said. 'Thanks for your help, Tod. See you sometime. 'Bye.'

On the way back to my hotel I was still wondering most of the time what had happened to L. A. Marley.

III

W E WERE A DAY'S SAIL FROM ST THOMAS, IN THE WEST
Indies, when the lady from New Orleans ('Call me Delia')
whispered: 'To come to the point, Doctor, I happen to know your
name isn't Sam Reiss – it's Doctor Kunz. If you'll agree to handle
the abortion of my baby, I'll double your usual fee.'

She had no need to whisper. We were alone in the palm garden
at the stern. The glass screens were open: if she had shouted,
the air drag would merely have carried her words back over the
ship's wake. No-one could have heard, save myself and the odd
flying-fish.

Over four months ago Marley had winded me by his remarks
about Lou. Delia's verbal punch from out of nowhere had nearly
the same effect. However, experience teaches. I partly rode the
blow, and recovered after a short silence during which Delia
watched me with anxious-hopeful, swimmy blue eyes.

'Who told you I was Doctor Kunz?'

She hesitated.

'I must know,' I said. 'I don't want this to go any further.'

'Well, it was your friend, that nice young Scotsman. You see,
him being a doctor and not a bit stuffy and *so* helpful… I thought
he might help me. But he said it was your line, not his, and you
were the best in the business. Safe as a bank, he said.'

'I see. But you're going home to New Orleans, Delia. I'm
continuing on the Panama Passage.'

'No, I'm stopping off at Havana. I thought you were too.
Look, I'm staying with old friends there. Lovely people and so

broadminded. Richer even than my husband. They have a *palace*. They'll give you a wonderful time if you'll—'

'Sorry, I can't. I'm not on a pleasure cruise. I've got an important job on my hands out there in the Pacific, and it can't wait.'

Disappointment and curiosity fought in her.

'Would it be prying to ask – who? I won't breathe a word to a soul, I promise.'

'Well… Have you heard of the Queen of Gardabonga?'

She nodded, her eyes brightening.

You're a born liar, I thought, because I've never heard of the Queen of Gardabonga.

'Then I don't have to say any more,' I said, quietly. 'Was that the dinner gong?'

It wasn't, but again she nodded. Then bounced out of her chair with commendable agility for one two months pregnant.

'Thank you, Doctor Kunz. You know, it helps a lot to learn that I'm not alone in my kind of trouble. Guess it happens to all of us. Don't worry about me. My friends in Havana have all sorts of contacts. They'll find someone. But I do wish it could have been you.'

She turned to go, then paused with a frown.

'But surely the Queen needs you right soon? Why didn't you take the rocket-plane from Europe instead of this slow old boat?'

'My nerves,' I said. 'I like to keep them steady for the sort of delicate operations I do. Space travel upsets my stomach.'

She smiled. 'I understand.'

I watched her hurry back along the enormous deck, clutching her new and tasty gobbet of gossip. She had old friends on this ship, too – lovely, broadminded people, I was sure.

Well, I hadn't told her any direct lies – unlike my friend, the helpful Scot.

It was Marley's idea that Thomson, Pettigue, and I travel incognito and by sea to Peniwak. We – I especially – had been through months of gruelling courses and hard cramming and were pretty beat up. Age and ability to learn aren't supposed to be correlated, according to the psychologists. They should try going back to college in their middle age.

I'd even gone by rocket-plane to Woomera for weeks of practical tests in a mock-up atomic ship which could have been carried out just as well at the Salisbury base.

It didn't help to have the gentlemen of the press in our hair most of the time.

One morning, Marley told us: 'Take-off day is three weeks hence. Tomorrow you three will embark at Southampton on the S.S. *Almeria*, ostensibly bound for Auckland. Actually, you'll be dropped off at Peniwak. Your passage has been booked under assumed names, so no-one will bother you. You're going to be cooped up in the *Endeavour* for quite a while, and it's necessary that you get properly adjusted to one another first.'

'You coming too?' I asked.

'I can't spare the time for sea trips. I'll take a rocket-plane.'

'So how do we learn to get adjusted to you?' I asked, pointedly.

Marley said, calmly: 'Doctor Thomson doesn't have to learn. He's been our family doctor for years, as his father was before him. As for you and Pettigue, all you have to learn is how to carry out my orders without question and we'll get along fine.'

'Will your daughter be coming with you – or with us?' I pursued.

'She will not be coming to Peniwak,' said Marley, with an extra twist to his disagreeable grin.

Thomson, the old friend of the family, smiled at my surprise. Obviously, he was *au fait* with family plans.

'For the simple reason,' went on Marley, 'that she's already there. She's been there for a month now.'

I had nothing to say to that, and Pettigue had nothing to say to anything. He was so incognito on the ship that I wasn't certain he was aboard until we were three days out. If he patronized the dining salon he must have merged with the other gnomes and elves in the fancy frescoes. More probably, he had his meals served in his cabin.

Anyhow I was sea-sick for two days and quite uninterested in other people. Thomson, who wasn't sick, I did get to know – rather better than I wished to.

He turned out to be The Man I Should Least Like to Trust.

Not that he was exactly Iago re-born: he was too petty by far. But beneath the gentlemanly charm, behind the quizzical blue eyes, was the character of a chimpanzee. I reckon the happiest days of his life were when he was a medical student. He was the ringleader of most of the hospital rags, and he never tired of telling me about them.

'I let the copper have that stinking cod's head smack in his rosebud mouth…'

'I made a fine show of helping her out of the fountain and all the while I was really shoving her back in…'

'Ever seen Eros with a bright blue nose? It wouldn't come off for weeks. *I* mixed that paint…'

Puerile as he was, he had the one necessary asset of the successful examinee: a good memory. So he'd accumulated a string of medical degrees. But I should hate to have him lance a boil on my backside. He took an almost feminine pleasure in stabbing people in the back, I found.

'The famous Colonel Marley, Master of Fox Hounds, a confidant of Premiers, the power behind the throne, snob extraordinary, is in fact just scum from the gutter,' he remarked one day.

'Like me, you mean?' I asked.

'Why, my father had to teach him what cutlery to use.'

'You wield a pretty useful knife yourself, Tommy.'

He grinned. 'I get you. But only a fool would flash one in Marley's face. He's a wild man, and I'm a diplomat. My family were diplomats first, doctors second. Marley carries on his family tradition, too: he comes from a long line of morons and fakes.'

'All the same, he's done better for himself than you have. Jealous?'

'Jealous of his luck, yes. It's nothing but luck, believe me.'

Thomson went on to tell me about Marley, some things I knew and others that I didn't. Marley had suffered from the chronic family poverty as a kid. He resented it because he held it was his rightful destiny to have been born rich. His grandfather had made a big strike in the Yukon rush but simple-mindedly allowed himself to be bamboozled out of it by legal trickery.

Therefore, Marley figured he'd been robbed of his inheritance. And that included entree to the big houses and exclusive clubs where all the people who matter forgather.

He was on the outside looking in, and he meant to get in.

He was obsessed by the idea of emulating his grandfather, making a lucky strike – but holding on to it. As a young man he went to West Africa, worked in goldfields, prospected. He struck gold, all right, but indirectly. He discovered nothing in the ground but plain dirt, but he discovered in himself a lucky streak – at paper gambling. First with cards, then with gold-mine shares.

After two years with pick and shovel, he owned nothing but the pick and shovel. After two months of speculation, he owned a gold-mine. He gained control of others, and inevitably moved into the circles of wealth and power where he felt he truly belonged.

He married a wealthy English aristocrat, and divorced her after fifteen years of misalliance.

'He pulled a real fast one there,' chuckled Thomson. 'She was as innocent as a lamb, but he bought false witnesses in bundles of a dozen. He was even awarded custody of the child.'

'Lou?'

'Of course. She was the only child.' Thomson looked at me suddenly. 'I'm talking too much, Franz. Don't repeat any of it, for your own sake. If it got back to Marley's ears... You could prove nothing, I'd deny everything, and Marley would believe me – because I'm a gentleman and you're not. And he'd crucify you.'

'Thanks, pal. You'd rather enjoy that, though, wouldn't you?'

'Anything for a laugh,' said Thomson, and caught sight of Pettigue sidling past. 'Hi, Pet, did you bag anything?'

At first Pettigue made as if to walk on. Then he stopped. Maybe he remembered it was his duty on this trip to work up a little team spirit. Reluctantly, he came over, jaws moving in slow time.

'To what are you referring, Doctor Thomson?' His voice was a squeak like a rusty key turning.

'Did you bag anything on that hunting trip you made – to the Mato Grosso?'

Pettigue stopped chewing. His brown face lightened a shade. He said, almost inaudibly: 'I have heard you boast of your memory, Doctor. But sometimes it's imprudent to remember what others forget.'

He slouched away.

Thomson laughed, then turned to me, opening his mouth to speak. I put my flat palm over it.

'Hush. You talk too much, like you said. I don't want to know what you've got against that poor little sap.'

Thomson pushed my hand away. 'Poor little nothing! You think my tongue viperish? I'm a grass-snake beside him. He's a black mamba. Be careful he doesn't strike at you – as well he may. And that's a solemn warning. Now, what about some poker? I'm not lucky at it, like Marley, but you won't catch me cheating. You can try, but you won't catch me...'

He was right. Instead he caught me – for plenty. The hell of it was that I knew he had cards up his sleeve, but I couldn't prove it. He knew I knew, and was enjoying tormenting me.

Call him a sadist and he would have felt insulted. He didn't see himself as cruel in any way. Dumping an old woman in a fountain wasn't cruel – only a funny joke. Looked at from the right angle, life was nothing more than one big party – and he was the life and soul of it.

I never found practical jokers funny at any time: merely bores who became violent irritants if they kept on with it. Thomson kept on with it. I discovered drawing-pins on chairs – the hard way. Once, my toothpaste turned out to be mustard in a camouflaged tube. I tangled with apple-pie beds.

I accepted it, grimly, glumly. Until this final gag of his persuading the fatuous Delia that I was a Doctor Kunz of unsavoury reputation.

Thomson, I decided, needed to be taught a lesson. I hadn't the inventiveness or the inclination to repay him in his own coin. That tit-for-tat game could go on forever. He needed a plain, old-fashioned poke on the nose.

I walked out of that palm garden, bent on violence, past other gardens. The salt sea breeze sent my tie flapping over my shoulder. I felt springy and fit. The rest and the fresh air had paid off. This new atomic-powered *Almeria* was a kind of floating sanatorium, I thought. No obtrusive superstructure, just the one small control dome and the radar mast. Acres of flowering gardens, shady arbours, colourful, winding walks – all made proof against Atlantic storms, if necessary, by the touching of a button.

If the *Endeavour* rode space as comfortably as the *Almeria* rode the seas, I should be a satisfied man.

I got to thinking about the *Endeavour* and almost forgot what I'd set forth to do. However, I passed within eye-shot of Thomson and he brought it on himself. He called: 'Franz – how about a spot of tennis? Over half an hour yet till dinner, dammit.'

I said: 'Sure, I'd like to limber up. But the courts are crowded. Let's have a spar in the gym instead.'

He looked surprised. 'That could be a bit comic. I'm in the middle-weight class. You're – what? Bantam?'

'Featherweight. So we'd look comic. So what? Give the folks a laugh. That's what you like to do, isn't it?'

He grinned. 'I'm on. It might be a laugh, at that.'

Actually, the gym turned out to be deserted, but I insisted we went through with it. I hadn't had the gloves on in years, but I was good in my day. I thought I had enough residual reflexes left to give him a steady working over.

The trouble was, he was good too. Also, years younger. Also, his reach exceeded mine. He kept, gently but firmly, poking me with a straight left, keeping me at a cool distance. I flailed away energetically, disturbing plenty of air but not him in the least. This waste of hard work amused him no end.

It infuriated me, as did anything which reflected upon my disadvantage in size. I kept trying to slip his lead and get to in-fighting but he was that much too clever. He blocked me constantly. Finally,

I stopped, and breathing hard, said: 'Do something about your shoe-lace.'

He looked down at his shoe-lace, which was neatly tied. Just as neatly as I caught him with a right uppercut. I gave it all I had left. He teetered on his heels, lost his balance, sat hard on the floor. Blood ran down his upper lip. His eyes were round, shocked.

'Funny?' I asked. 'Good for a laugh?'

'You little swine!' he exclaimed, thickly, and a small spray of blood came with the words. 'I'm going to flatten you for that.'

He started to get to his feet.

'I didn't hit you,' I said. 'It was that bastard, Doctor Kunz.'

'Oh.' He paused, reflecting, on one knee. 'So Delia tackled you?'

'She did. Now, look here, Tommy, I'm fed up with your silly jokes. In future, if you try any on me again I'll hit back hard, above or below the belt. Once I get you on my ship I can make it tough for you in a hundred ways, believe me. So lay off. Try to grow up, for Pete's sake. You're in long trousers now.'

He got up. 'All right, Franz, we'll call it quits. But get this: I never liked you much, and now I like you less. Socially, my friend, we're worlds apart. If you have any further need to communicate with me, do so privately. Don't speak to me in front of my friends; they're decent people.'

There was one wordless answer to that, and I was coarse enough to make it.

'Sorry to be so vulgar,' I said. 'Lack of breeding, you know. If I want you, I'll send for you to come to my cabin. And you'd better come, so long as I remain Captain.'

I walked away.

My dignity sagged a bit when I discovered myself entering the dining salon still wearing boxing gloves. That head-on clash had upset me more than I cared to admit. Character is destiny, and it seemed my destiny always to be friendless, while my enemies increased and multiplied.

That hadn't mattered during my career as a lone pilot. But now I'd been placed in charge of a crew and it was my responsibility to mould them into a unit – even if it meant a fight to change my own character.

Unenthusiastically, I resolved to achieve some sort of contact with Pettigue. Perhaps behind the reserve lay hidden a lonely heart crying silently for response. One had to try to melt the cold barrier of shyness.

I came upon him one evening at sunset, leaning on the rail, watching the sea-reflected glory in the west.

'The real thing makes most paintings of it look pretty drab, eh?' I ventured, amiably.

His lips parted slightly. It looked as though I'd won a response. I waited for it. He spat a wad of chewing gum into the sea and shambled off.

Maybe he didn't like art. Or maybe he did.

Some time later, as the big ship crawled through the widened Panama Canal, I saw him staring away to the south.

I said: 'Crazy, isn't it? Here's us setting out to explore the moon, while, way down south there, thousands of square miles of Mother Earth still remain largely unexplored.'

He began to tremble, with fear or anger, or both.

Too late I recalled that the area of the Mato Grosso was a sore spot with him for some unknown reason. He gave me no chance to change the subject: he slunk away.

My third and last attempt came next day.

It was very hot and humid with it. I was looking for a shady spot in one of the gardens when I noticed Pettigue asleep in a chair in a little fern grove. His hands were folded across an open book on his lap. I went quietly up behind him and looked over his shoulder, curious to discover his literary tastes.

The book was the complete works of Shakespeare, open at *Henry IV,* and the first two lines of one of Hotspur's speeches were underlined in pencil:

> *By heavens, methinks it were an easy leap*
> *To pluck bright honour from the pale-faced moon.*

In the margin had been planted a bracketed exclamation mark.

Pettigue's small hands obscured the rest of the page. His fingers limply held a pencil. So almost certainly he was the underliner.

I considered mentally a few opening gambits:

'Shakespeare always had a word for it, didn't he?'

'D'you think Shakespeare wrote Shakespeare?'

'I rather prefer the historical plays myself, too.'

I meant to cough discreetly, but overdid it and barked in his ear like a seal. He literally sprang awake, dropping the pencil, clutching the book, and spun around on his feet. I never suspected he could move so fast. His nerves were as taut as violin strings. He stared at me wildly.

'I guess you don't think it's such an easy leap to pluck honour from the moon,' I said, out of the blue, surprising myself.

He raised the book as if he were going to throw it at my head.

'If you and Thomson don't stop tormenting me, I'll take steps to make you,' he said, in a furious squeak. He slammed the book under his arm, and this time made off at a near-run.

There and then I abandoned the idea of trying to appear a normal, pleasant person. I had to accept myself as I was, even if no-one else could accept me. For the rest of my life I should continue to say precisely the wrong thing, touch people on the raw, and generally be unpopular. I had a natural gift for it.

The *Almeria* broke out into the broad Pacific and swept south-west towards the Tropic of Capricorn. She was carrying a thousand souls and I was on speaking terms with hardly any of them. Yet, in contrast, travelling in the *Endeavour* would be like taking a ride in a rocket-bomb with a leary fuse.

Consider. In one common cage would be confined:

A brutal megalomaniac.

His neurotic, unpredictable, self-willed daughter.

A mystery man, or worm on the turn, with persecution mania.

A spiteful snob-cum-schoolboy idiot hoaxer.

My difficult self.

A cat (?).

It made me realize what overwhelming push and power Marley had. Who else could have got away with such blatantly bad selection of personnel? It was a sackful of Kilkenny cats. It was like the cast list of one of Sartre's more cannibalistic plays. Each of us was blighted by neuroses and infantilism.

The *Endeavour* was going to be far removed from Mountbatten's 'happy and efficient ship'. If I could persuade myself that its maiden voyage was going to be other than disastrous, then I was a real dab at kidding myself.

I, WHO HAD FROM SPACE SO MANY TIMES SURVEYED THE whole Pacific almost at a glance, had never sailed it.

Peniwak was my first tropical island.

The *Almeria* laid to a mile out beyond the spreading coral reefs. All silver fire in the morning sunlight, the *Endeavour*, amid a court of service gantries, towered over the palm trees.

This side of the island showed no other sign of habitation. The beach of white sand ran bare to the flanking coral promontories. Long John Silver stumping along it, Robinson Crusoe building a boat on it, would have looked right at home. But spacemen there were anachronisms.

The launch Thomson, Pettigue, and I were in, with our baggage, cut an ephemeral furrow in the glass-like sea, blue as dye, as it slid around to a reefless bay on the farther shore.

Rounding the northern headland was like turning some fourth-dimensional corner into Bermuda. Here, suddenly, was a port, jetties, wharves, cranes, backed by rising steps of bungalows and starkly white office blocks. All clean and new, as if the polythene wrappings were stripped off only yesterday.

It was there to serve only one passing purpose: the launching of the first atomic-powered space-ship. If the take-off was successful, it would demonstrate that remote islands weren't necessary for such launchings. If something went wrong and the *Endeavour* became an atomic bomb, then that also would be the finish of little Peniwak.

One way or another, this was destined to become a ghost town.

Just now, it was well populated, and most of the population was waiting on the quay to meet us. The moment our launch was moored, our period of privacy ended.

There began a day-long round of introductions, press interviews, conferences, drinks... We were shown our apartments, the club, the firing control set-up, and the *Endeavour* itself. The ship was even roomier than I'd imagined, and that was a good thing: the occupants would welcome any space they could put between themselves.

We inspected the deep shelters where everybody else would be skulking while we endured the count-down out on the launching pad.

We met everyone except the one person I was curious – but not anxious – to meet again. I had not seen Lou since that one unsettling encounter with her, and I'd had no occasion to revisit Marley's house. Anyhow, she had been here on Peniwak for some six weeks now.

I'd thought about her, on and off, and she remained an enigma. I hoped she'd been brushing up on her work. The Americans and the Russians had been digging around sporadically in their respective allotted segments of the moon, and if they had settled the difficult question of whether there had once been life on our satellite they hadn't publicly announced it.

If Lou was as good as she'd been cracked up to be, Europe, although only third in the moon race, might yet be the first to come up with the long-awaited answer to that one. The *Endeavour's* trip could be more scientifically significant than the brief visit and look-see scheduled.

I was still the world's worst mixer, barring Pettigue, and when evening approached I was inwardly screaming to get away from people and their stupid questions and opinions. The crowded clubroom had become my idea of hell.

The john had another way out and I took it. I knew there'd be no sanctuary in my apartment, so I hiked across the island to the deserted beach I'd seen. Apart from a few crabs, it was still deserted. I settled myself comfortably on it and lit a cigar.

Behind me the sun was sinking into the palms, but still made the dome of the *Almeria* out at sea an arc of brightness. She would be resuming her journey to Auckland later tonight.

Presently I noticed a dark head in the sea in that direction, making its way fast towards my beach. I presumed that there was a body attached, and cursed. Solitude seemed unattainable.

The swimmer had long black hair and was probably female. The matter of sex was settled definitely when she walked out of the surf some fifty yards to my left. Tanned, slim, beautifully proportioned, straight-backed but graceful, she stepped up the beach, chose a spot and lay relaxed. Usually I'm not all that fascinated by the female form, but I found it hard work pretending this one wasn't there.

At last I shut my eyes to prevent myself from looking out of the corners of them.

I'd even begun to think of something else, when Lou's unmistakable Girton College voice spoke above my head: 'Is there any pleasure in smoking if you can't see the smoke, Captain Brunel?'

That was an eye-opener, all right. A mouth-opener, too. My cigar fell clean out. I sat up, grabbing for it. The bronze beauty was standing legs astride, over my feet, wearing a brief costume and an unlit cigarette. Her wet hair hung lankly down to her corset model's bosom.

It was Lou, sure enough, minus many pounds and plus this rich golden tan. The transformation was astonishing.

As I appeared unable to answer her question, she asked another: 'Do you have a light?'

I located my lighter and flipped it.

She bent over me, to edge her cigarette into the flame. I was offered – and accepted – another view of the bosom from another, more revealing, angle.

She straightened and said: 'I've become one hell of a smoker since I gave up eating.'

I suppose a good conversationalist could have made a reasonable rejoinder to that. I couldn't muster one.

She blew smoke and stared at me through it with those jet-black eyes. Then she murmured: 'I also seem to be acquiring the habit of talking to myself. Well, thanks, Captain. Good evening.'

Unhurriedly, with the ease of movement of a cat, she stepped away.

'Don't go,' my voice said, all by itself.

She stopped.

'How are you?' I asked, lamely.

'Fine, thanks.'

'That's good. And – er – Carmack?'

'He's fine, too.'

I was drying up fast, but the *Almeria* gave two long hoots: the signal for the landing party to prepare to return. It gave me another small hook.

'You swam out to the ship?'

She nodded. 'Around it. I didn't go aboard – merely wanted a closer look at it. I've not seen one of that type.'

'She's really something,' I said, and began describing the *Almeria's* special attractions. Lou was interested and quietly sat beside me.

The conversation flourished. She asked me how Marley was when I last saw him. She referred to him as 'my father', never as 'daddy'. And she'd dropped that way of describing herself in the third person. I felt myself in the presence of a sensible, adult, well-balanced person who might very well have written *Organic Structures in Carbonaceous Meteorites*, even if she did look like Gabrielle Gavin.

This, I thought, was how she must have been when she wrote that masterpiece.

Again I found myself wondering: what happened? And what had happened since to cause the reversion to normal?

The landing party's launch hummed back across an empurpled sea as the sun prepared for its quick tropic dive.

And all at once the stars were out, while we were still talking and smoking. She hadn't dried herself and didn't seem worried about it.

She spoke of her biochemical research work and of what we might find on the moon. I was impressed. This was the authoritative article: a cool, methodical, dedicated scientific mind.

Yet she was a philosopher, too. She alluded to the antiscientist, D. H. Lawrence, and his disbelief that the moon was like Earth grown cold – instead, he said, it was 'a globe of dynamic substance... coagulated upon a vivid pole of energy.' She said he believed there was no such thing as dead matter, that it was as intrinsically alive as the human mind which interacted with it through the mere act of perception.

She lay back on the warm sand and declaimed to the heavens:

> *No, no, ye stars! there is no death with you,*
> *No languor, no decay! languor and death,*
> *They are with me, not you! ye are alive –*
> *Ye, and the pure dark ether where ye ride...*

'*Empedocles on Etna* – Matthew Arnold,' she informed me – necessarily.

'You're trying to kid me that you're well-read,' I said, and the subject switched to literature. One thing soon became plain: she was well-read. Strange that the coarse, facile Marley should breed such a daughter. The sensitivity must have come from her mother's side.

'What kind of person is your mother?' I asked, on impulse.

She made no answer for a time. Then: 'She's dead,' she said, quietly. 'Let her rest in peace.'

I shut up. We lay silently for a while, looking up at the stars. I thought: above each man's head, as he walks this planet Earth, stretches an infinity of space containing an infinity of possibilities. But his mind is finite. As he strains it to encompass infinity, sooner or later something must give. As the circle of knowledge widens, inexorably the boundary of ignorance lengthens.

Beyond limits, in sub-zero temperatures, in the sub-atomic world, in the reaches of extra-galactic space, things began to fail to tie in with the laws of man-made logic or human reason. Or even with observable laws of nature.

Man is a born over-reacher. In those dangerous places he is destined to go mad.

At which moment, on this timeless, silent beach, Lou went mad.

She flung herself on top of me, clasped me in a bear-hug and crushed her lips passionately against mine. My nose felt quite flat and I couldn't breathe. I thought my ribs were cracking. I tried to push her away. Her body was still damp in this vaporous atmosphere, and my hands kept slipping.

She felt warm and firm, and she was as strong as a wrestler. Whatever she'd inherited from her mother, she had her father's physical vitality.

I wished I had some of it. I'd lost this bout and would soon lose consciousness if she didn't let up. At last she used her lips just to speak. She said, in a low, fierce voice: 'I love you, little Captain Brunel, and you're going to marry me – or I'll break your neck.'

I gasped: 'I think… you've already… broken my neck.'

She laughed – that warm, sexy laugh I remembered. Only tonight there was even more animal in it.

A thrill ran through me: a mixture of excitement and fear. The excitement was the lure of new adventure. The fear was the threat of entanglement and loss of freedom.

'Do you love me?' Lou asked.

'Well, frankly – no.'

'I'll teach you to,' she said, reassuringly. 'Don't let it worry you.'

'Thanks a lot, Lou. You've taken a load off my mind. How about taking the load off my chest, too? I'm suffocating.'

She kissed me again, then relaxed her grip. I wriggled free and stood up, panting. A thin shower of sand from my clothing sprinkled her thighs and midriff as she lay there smiling up at me. The tropical stars were blazing and I could see the white glimmer of her teeth.

Lust and myself played a short, tough game of catch-as-catch-can. I won – just. The deciding factor was the knowledge that the *Endeavour* was scheduled to take off in seven days flat. To be fully in control of the ship I had to be fully in control of myself.

I said, quite sharply: 'I'm going back to the settlement. You coming?'

'Yes, Franz – it *is* Franz?'

I remained silent as she rose languidly. She collected a few odds and ends she'd brought with her in a waterproof bag. No clothes: apparently she walked around in a bathing suit most of the time – hence the tan.

The way back was tangential to the circular clearing where the *Endeavour*, only partially lit by a couple of arcs, stood like some strange monument. The black shape of my cabin, perched on high, looked like a hole in the Milky Way. Lower, there were faint tappings and scrapings from within the fat tubular ring which bulged like a spare tyre on the central cone: the technicians would never cease re-checking until blast-off.

Lou said: 'It crossed my mind that if your cabin had been fixed to the main axis and a coelostat installed to counteract the rotating field of vision...'

She criticized the whole design of the *Endeavour*, brilliantly. It was unsettling. I couldn't adapt myself to the sharp switches of this multiple personality. Here again was the cool, logical scientist – as though she hadn't a gland in her body.

Anyhow, I wasn't in the mood for talking shop now. I'd been offered plenty to drink during the day but little to eat. I was hungry, and presently I said so.

'The canteen's lousy here,' said Lou. 'The food is even worse than the service, which is damn nigh incredible. Have supper at my place. I can do you anything from a steak to an omelette.'

'Thanks all the same. But I feel the canteen's the lesser risk, and I'm not referring to the cooking.'

'Good heavens, Franz, I thought you were the kind of a man who could defend himself.'

'So did I,' I said.

We came to her bungalow. She pushed open the door, switched on the hall lamp, and beckoned me in. Silhouetted against the light her figure was eye-catching. I was reminded that I, at least, had glands.

Don't be a fool, I told myself...

All right, fool, in you go, I told myself.

I went in and fell over Mack, the cat.

'You brought that animal all the way out here?'

'Naturally – you don't think he swam here? You two had better make friends: you'll be seeing a lot of each other. Don't you think it's nice he'll be with us on the trip? It'll give the three of us something to talk over on the long wet evenings by the fireside. Mack will really be one of the family.'

'What family?'

'Why, the Brunels, of course.'

She was in the lounge now. I sighed and followed her in.

'Pour yourself a drink – I'll be getting dressed,' she said.

I poured myself a whisky of sufficient depth to gladden the eye even of her old man. 'Thank the lord for that,' I said, and I wasn't thinking of the drink.

The last of it was warming my gut when the door-bell rang.

'Come right in,' I said, as if I owned the place.

I should have been less hospitable. Thomson entered, at various angles: he'd been drinking, too, but for longer than me. He aimed with drunken deliberation, and just made his target: a divan.

He became aware of me. 'Stap me, it's Brunel. I'm not talking to you, Brunel.'

'That's right,' I said.

'What are you doing here in Lou's private shack, Brunel?'

'Just not being talked to – remember?'

'You don't belong here.'

'Do you?'

'I've known Lou since she was a kid. I'm a friend of the family, you know.'

'I know. I'm not.'

'Then get out, you dirty little half-breed.'

I never hit a drunk man unless I'm drunk too. I was a long way from being drunk. But I could work at it. I poured myself another stiff one.

Lou emerged from her bedroom in a night-dress as opaque as tissue paper. No dressing-gown. Thomson goggled at her. I was glad she wasn't silhouetted against the light this time.

'Hello, Tommy,' she said. 'Would you like some supper too? I'm just going to cook the Captain some.'

He sat up slowly. 'I see you're dressed for kitchen work, Lou. What dish are you intending to serve up to the Captain – yourself?'

I decided rules were only made to be broken, and I would hit him, after all. I started out, but Lou stepped between us.

'Ignore it, Franz – he's my ex-husband.'

It seems to me that any time I start in to hit anybody, somehow I get hit first, if only by surprise.

My shock-absorbers were more or less run in now, and I said quite soon: 'He shouldn't talk to you that way.'

'He always did: that's why he's my ex-husband.'

Thomson said, thickly: 'She collects ex-husbands, Franzy boy. And it's as plain as hell the collecting bug has bitten her again – she's in training for the hunt. I heard from her old man that she was shedding the avoirdupois and getting into trim for the chase. Some day soon now some unlucky fellow will be marked down, and – wham! He'll be wearing a whole set of tigress's claws in his back.'

I finished my second drink at a gulp.

Lou said: 'It won't be like that at all this time, Tommy. Franz and I have complementary personalities. We'll gravitate together. We can't help ourselves – it's a law of nature.'

Thomson sagged back in the divan. It was his turn to be socked by surprise.

'*Franz* and you! That pompous little runt?'

Then he laughed weakly. 'Give me a drink, for Pete's sake.' I passed him one, after I'd poured myself a third. He swallowed half, and said: 'When the Colonel hears about his new prospective son-in-law he'll beat the *Endeavour* to it: he'll blow the island apart.'

I began and finished my last drink. Then I said: 'On the remote chance that it may interest anyone, I should like to make an announcement. Simply this: I am a bachelor. I like being a bachelor. I intend to remain one. To dream may be a lovely thing, but in future will all dreamers please include me out of their fantasies. Thank you and good-night.'

I made for the door.

'Franz, you're forgetting your supper,' said Lou, evenly. 'Please stay for it – I'm looking forward to practising my cooking on you. It's especially true in your case that the way to a man's heart is through his stomach: you're too thick-headed to listen to reason.'

I looked back at her. She was regarding me indulgently, tolerantly, with a sort of to-understand-all-is-to-forgive-all expression. Her presumptuousness was infuriating.

'Give my supper to the cat,' I snapped.

'Franz,' said Thomson, over his glass, 'it's no good, you know. You're a dead duck. When Lou makes up her mind, she gets her way. I've never known her fail.'

'There's always a first time,' I said, and walked out.

Mack was crouching sphinx-like on the hall-stand. He looked as if he were biding his time to pounce, too.

I spent a hungry night. In the small hours I had to face it: I wasn't hungry only for food. Over and over again my mind's eye kept viewing the same strip of memory film: Lou emerging like Venus from the sea.

I would have to shut my mind's eye tight and run for my life.

The rocket-plane shrieked over Peniwak and made a sea-landing just over the dark blue horizon.

Within an hour, Marley had the crew of the *Endeavour* on parade for inspection.

To Thomson: 'Everything under control, Tommy?'

As if Thomson was his deputy.

To Pettigue: 'Stop chewing the cud. Throw that gum away. The *Endeavour* isn't a cattle-boat.'

To me: 'Don't look so worried, man – the ship will be easy to handle.'

I wasn't thinking about the ship at that time.

To Lou: 'Nice – very nice. You really meant it, then. Okay, who's the man?'

'Captain Brunel, Father.'

Straight from wintry London, Marley hadn't much colour when he arrived. Now, suddenly, he acquired plenty, mostly red and purple.

'Leave the funny jokes to Tommy,' he said, at last, but remained in a state of apoplectic inquiry.

'I'm not joking, Dad.'

He rounded on me. 'So that's why you looked worried, Brunel.'

'Yes, that's why.'

'You may be more worried yet. Lou, come with me. We'll have a little talk about this.'

'Pure waste of time,' said Lou, indifferently, but strolled away beside him.

Thomson said, maliciously: 'The big bang is coming your way.'

I was as spiteful. 'Didn't your marriage break up with a big bang?'

'No, only a whimper. It died away. The old man tried to patch it up. But I wasn't married to him.'

'What went wrong?'

'None of your business, Brunel. But it'll probably happen to you, too. Lou's an idealist – she disillusions easy.'

He sauntered off parade. I was left with Pettigue, who stood hunched like a query mark. He put his question into words. 'Do you think we'll be wanted any more?'

I looked at him. And thought: who would want you at any time, you queer little man? And reflected: maybe you're lucky at that. You'll never have a predatory female breathing down your neck. Your life's your own – for what it's worth.

'I doubt it,' I said. 'Get lost quietly.'

Marley didn't send for me till next morning, the day before blast-off. There was a heady smell of new paint in the office he needed for no more than forty-eight hours. The big bang turned out to be a strictly controlled explosion.

'My daughter has some odd ideas about you, Captain.'

'Very odd.'

'Forget them.'

'I'm trying to.'

'What do you mean by that?'

'I mean your daughter is a disturbing influence. She disturbs me, and I don't want to be disturbed.'

'I see. Well, keep your mind on your job. If she attempts to distract you further, inform me and I'll clamp down on her. She's headstrong, but I can handle her. I'm the only man who can.'

I might have made a superfluous comment but I didn't get the chance. The door was flung open and lost inches of new paint in a collision with the side of the desk. Lou stormed in.

'Father, Mack's dying. What do you know about it?'

Marley flushed. 'Are you implying I should know something about it?'

'I'm not implying – I'm asking.'

'All right. I know nothing.'

'I think you're lying. He's been poisoned.'

Marley gave me a curt nod of dismissal. I dismissed. I don't know who slammed the door behind me, but it did little to muffle the sound of the first-class row beginning in there.

At the porch I encountered Thomson. He looked excited yet apprehensive. He asked: 'Is the Colonel in there?'

'Yes, but I wouldn't advise you to barge in right now. He's having a spat with Lou. Seems her cat's in a bad way.'

'I know. She asked me to look at it. I think it's got some tropical disease. It's paralysed and going fast.'

He addressed his remarks to the nobody standing beside me. Therefore, I treated them as suspect. I tried to look into his eyes but they dodged every which way.

The ill-used office door banged again. Lou came pushing between us, tears flowing to her chin. She ran towards her hut.

People seemed prone to tell me nothing was my business, and I was willing to agree this was none of mine. I walked away, ever more slowly, until I came to an indecisive stop. Damn the woman! Why should it worry me to see her crying?

Without conscious volition, I drifted towards her bungalow. The door was ajar. I could hear her sobbing. I went in hesitantly.

On the bright red counterpane of the bed the black shape of Carmack, paws extended fore and aft, lay still. Lou lay beside him, her face buried in her arms.

I felt the cat. Its muscles were hard and knotted. It felt warm but it was dead. I patted Lou's shoulder gently. I wanted to express sympathy but could find no words.

Muffledly, she said: 'He was a stupid cat but I loved him.'

I said, quietly: 'But he couldn't have come with us, you know.'

She lifted her head, turned a tear-stained face up at me.

'Go away, you bloody fool.'

'Sorry.' I turned to go. Her hand darted forth swift as an adder's tongue, caught my wrist in a fierce grip and dragged me down beside her on the bed. Her arms locked around me and she kissed me hungrily. This time I didn't resist. I found myself responding.

'You're all I have left to love now,' she murmured, presently.

She began undoing the buttons of my shirt. One was stubborn; she tore it off impatiently. I felt myself going down into roaring waters...

Before I was quite lost I kicked out and struggled to the surface of consciousness. I staggered back from the bed.

'You were right, Lou. I'm a bloody fool. I'll go away.'

Leaning on her elbows, in silence she watched me go. I hadn't the least intention of obeying Marley's instructions and reporting her behaviour. I'd always fought my own battles. But I knew this was going to be the toughest battle yet.

V

Burton's multi-volume *Conquest of the Moon* gives a well-documented account of the *Endeavour's* take-off. His data is accurate and comprehensive. Anyone predominantly interested in the technicalities of the maiden voyage of the first nuclear spaceship will already have drunk their fill at this source.

There's no point to my plagiarizing his work. He's a first-rate scientific journalist, and more. He can write for the expert without losing the common touch. He has the knack of the dramatist, and often his prose becomes a kind of poetry.

He puts across the mounting tension of that day when little Peniwak became the white-hot focus of world attention. His book is first-hand reportage – from the bunker. And it's good second-hand reportage from verbal accounts, including my own.

However, he couldn't tell what he didn't know. There was a deal more tension in the ship than he or the world at large dreamed of.

The main purpose of this narrative is to reveal the crew's personal stresses and set the record clear from that angle.

For the rest, refer to Burton.

It was in the region of my two-hundredth take-off. The chemical booster lifted us to a height of a hundred or so miles with no trouble, all systems Go.

I watched the instruments and disengaged the booster myself, a fraction of a second before ground control would have done it. It parted from us with a slight last kick. I pressed the HAPU start button before any darned robot mechanism had time to collect its wits.

I was just showing my independence, of course. Deep down, though, I felt I was putting out a flag for humanity. If we let ourselves get slack we should end up several jumps behind the machines.

We'd been under nearly three G from the booster, but when that thrust ceased and the gentle acceleration of the HAPU took over, conditions reverted to roughly normal gravity. I aimed to keep the ship at that constant acceleration until it reached escape velocity.

It meant that down there under me the Marleys, Thomson, and Pettigue were walking on the walls of their living quarters, for the ship was not yet revolving. The time for spinning would come when the *Endeavour* ceased to accelerate and merely coasted, for then a non-grav. condition would obtain.

It was a pity that Zignawitsch was objectionable as a person, for it was clear that the HAPU was designed by a genius. It did precisely what it was supposed to do. I had to admit that the hydrogen efflux, steadily reeling out like silk, drove us up a path noticeably less bumpy than the kind I remembered from experience with the often wayward chemical fuels.

I was alone in my cabin. The TV screens showed the great blue curve of Earth and the blackness of space. The radio crackled with voices, crisply darting in and out of each other's way, like a sort of audio square dance.

All our readings were being telemetered back, and I had little to do, radio-wise, beyond reporting from time to time that we were still on course and still in one piece. I imagined that Marley, on his separate wave-length, had far more to say.

Presently, there was a scraping of feet in the tube connecting my cabin with the body of the ship. The rungs there ran completely around the inside of the tube, forming so many steel hoops. At the moment, it didn't matter, but when the ship started revolving that tube would become the transition point between some degree of artificial weight and none at all, between motion and stasis. The circular rungs should ease negotiation of the change-over.

I wasn't expecting visitors yet, least of all Pettigue. He scrambled into the cabin like a small white ape. The boffins had designed tight-fitting white tunics and breeches for ship-wear. They suited Lou and Thomson, who had figures. The rest of us looked like comic characters in a ballet.

Pettigue was extremely nervous. A facial tic gave him a momentary sneer every few seconds. His right shoulder kept jerking. His cheeks were the colour of weak tea. He was under intense internal pressure and it made him almost voluble.

'I can't stand it down there any longer, Captain Brunel. Would I be in the way if I stayed here for a while?'

'Not at all. What's bothering you?'

He perched on the edge of a couch, clenching and unclenching his fists on his thighs. There was sweat on his brow.

Looking anywhere but at me, he said: 'I've never been into space before.'

'Oh, is that all? I was scared the first time, too, though I'd been trained for it. But there's nothing to be scared about now, Pettigue. The blast-off was the worst part. That's over, and we're through the first of the Van Allen belts with no trouble.' I was trying to kid myself, too. The landing on the moon was going to be the worst part, for me. That was the one major operation I'd not done before. Despite all my experience I would have to face a scarifying first time, too.

'It's all right for you, Captain. You're not a coward. I am.'

'If you were a coward, Pet, you wouldn't have come on this trip. And I seem to remember you've been on one or two pretty hazardous expeditions before this.'

He made a noise between a bitter laugh and an exclamation of disgust. 'Sure, but I had to kick myself into them from behind. You see, I felt I had to prove myself or else give up pretending I was a man. I proved myself, all right: I proved myself a coward. I was scared every minute of every hour.'

'Somebody said "Show me a man who doesn't know fear, and I'll show you a fool." If you're afraid but you face it nevertheless, then you're a brave man.'

Again that sound of bitter self-loathing.

'But, I didn't face it, Captain. I ran away.'

'Oh. Was that on the Mato Grosso trip?'

'Do you have to pretend you don't know?'

I said: 'I'm not pretending anything. I've a vague recollection of hearing something about it years ago, that's all. But I seldom read newspapers. I've spent a lot of time in space, and what passes for news on Earth doesn't much interest me any more.'

'I thought you knew. I thought Doctor Thomson would have refreshed your memory, anyhow – *he* remembers, all right, and he doesn't want me to forget it. As if I could! That Scotch bastard suspects the truth, and you bet he's passed his suspicions on to the Colonel. Are you sure he said nothing to you?'

'He tried to tell me about it, but I shut him up. You're quite right: he likes to see people squirm. It's a characteristic he shares with the Colonel.'

'Colonel Marley is a born bully, but at least he's a man,' said Pettigue. 'Thomson's a different kind of bully. I doubt if he were born that way. I guess it's a disease he picked up at school. He was bullied, so he aped the bullies in his own mean little way. If you can't beat them, join them, and be on the safe side.'

'You could be right.'

'I was the only survivor of that Mato Grosso expedition,' said Pettigue, going off at a tangent. 'That is, apart from Thorneycroft, our medico. He went down with fever – we had to send him back to Cuibá. The rest of us went on into the forest. It was unexplored country beyond the area where Colonel Fawcett vanished. So far beyond that even the speculators in San Páo hadn't found the boob who would buy a square mile of it. The Indians daily grew more threatening. They scared our bearers into quitting us altogether. Then at last they made a full-scale attack on our camp. It was our guns against their arrows – poisoned arrows. There were four of us… until I dropped my gun and ran.'

'I see. And you think the Indians might have been beaten off if you'd had the guts to stay.'

'No,' said Pettigue, 'I don't. I ran partly to save my own skin. Partly because I couldn't be a damn bit of use. I'm not a bad shot. Twice I had an Indian in my sights. Each time my finger just froze to the trigger. I just couldn't kill a man, not even a man who was trying to kill me. I was brought up to believe all life is sacred.'

'In which case, what have you to be ashamed of? Ethically, if not literally, you stuck to your guns. Why do you get angry every time you're reminded of the incident?'

He pounded at his thighs with his fists and squeaked despairingly: 'I don't know. I don't know. They gave me a decoration when I got back to London. Maybe it's the irony of that which burns me up when I think about it now. A decoration for cowardice! I still feel I've got to prove myself – *really* prove myself. Maybe I was taught the wrong things. Maybe you can only prove you're a man by killing another man.'

'Rubbish!' I snapped. 'Sheer gangster talk. If you want to prove you're not a coward you've got to learn to control yourself. And stick to your own beliefs. Put that juvenile nonsense about killing right out of your mind. There are too many violent apes around as it is. Lord, you're supposed to be an intelligent man. I shouldn't have to preach. Grow up and conduct your own life, darn you.'

Grow up. It was advice I could give to every person in this ship, not least to myself.

Pettigue rested his head on his fists and was silent.

I turned my attention to the instrument panel. Presently, I said: 'In a few minutes I shall cut the motor. That means there'll be a state of free fall in this cabin. You may find it unpleasant. I advise you to go below: pretty soon it'll be normal grav. down there.'

Pettigue said, quietly: 'You're advising me to dodge something unpleasant. Yet you just told me to grow up, which means learning to face unpleasantness.'

'Only if it's necessary to face it. But it's not necessary for you to remain in here, is it?'

He got up slowly.

'I'll go below. Believe me, I'd rather stay here. It's a sight more unpleasant down there. The atmosphere is terrible. They keep fighting. They were tearing my nerves to shreds. But it's necessary to live with them. That's my duty, I was told. I'll go back.'

I felt a depression heading my way. 'What are they fighting about?'

'The Colonel found a dead cat in his bunk. It's Miss Marley's – she put it there. He blew up. She flared back at him and accused him of killing it.'

'So Mack came along with us, after all. One black cat who hasn't brought us any luck. Will that pair ever stop fighting?'

'Not in this life,' said Pettigue, with a strange emphasis.

Or maybe it was just my imagination which charged his words with strange emphasis. He was working his way back down the connecting tube, so I didn't see his eyes. Maybe I missed nothing, anyhow: his eyes weren't his most expressive feature.

Duly, I cut the motor. Acceleration ceased. My moment of panic came and passed, but the breathless biliousness lingered. I floated between hand-holds, operating the side-jets to rotate the main body of the ship. When I hit the correct r.p.m. figure – and it took some doing – I turned off the jets. The ship, except for my cabin, would continue to rotate through inertia.

I made my reports, received some stereotyped congratulations (I guess they were saving their real enthusiasm for the big man, Marley) and reluctantly went below to check the artificial grav. in the general quarters.

It was normal, all right. So was the general atmosphere: they were still fighting.

Lou was nursing the stark body of Mack and glaring like a much wilder cat at her father and Dr Thomson. Pettigue had retreated to the far side of the big circular tube. He was out of their sight but not out of earshot: the tube was like a whispering gallery. Echoes of shouts hit you in the back of the neck while you were still rocking from the frontal blast.

A dizziness came upon me. It was not merely an effect of the sudden return to feeling the weight of my bones and flesh. Nor was it the strange perspective. I stood on a valley floor, as it were, while the others stood at odd angles on the gentle rises on either side of me. Nor did it arise from seeing the stars now swinging past the portholes and Earth oscillating like a balloon in a high wind.

It was the sheer psychic pressure of the presence of these people.

Yuri Gagarin, the first spaceman, prophesied back in the 'sixties that the automatically piloted space-ships of the future would permit anyone to be a space-traveller, irrespective of training or qualifications.

True, but I doubted that he visualized travellers like these. They would have rocked any boat anywhere.

'Your trouble is that you've always had everything you wanted, you ungrateful brat.' Marley's face was dark red: he looked as though he had been standing on his head.

'Especially your own way, Lou,' Thomson added. He was so pale that his freckles looked black.

'You two make me sick!' Lou shouted. 'You're just a pair of connivers. Tommy there is itching to grab a share of our family's money-bags. And you, dear Father, are just dying to be related to *his* illustrious family. My feelings don't matter a damn to you. Okay, leave me out of it altogether. Marry each other. You're ideally suited.'

Marley raised his great fist threateningly. Lou hurled the dead cat at him, and missed.

At that, I became as disgusted and angry as any of them.

I barked: 'Pipe down, all of you! I've had all I'm going to take of your family rows. We're supposed to be here to do a job – together. A lot of people have sweated blood to build this ship and get us here. Not one of them fell down on their job. But we'll fall down on ours if this doesn't stop. Remember, we represent something. Not just Europe and the Commonwealth, but all mankind.'

'Ta-ra-ra-ra.' It was Thomson's derisive imitation of a bugle.

I could have hit him. But I had to set them an example. I controlled myself.

'Now, for Pete's sake, let's try to be adult and reasonable and make some effort to pull together,' I said, trying to sound adult and reasonable.

'I told her not to bring that cat, so she brought it,' said Marley, grinning with rage. 'And stuck it among my blankets. The thing smells to high heaven.'

Lou's anger changed to the cold kind. 'I told you, back there, I was bringing Mack, and I meant it. If he's dead, that's because you killed him – you and Tommy. I would take a bet it was your very own idea, and you got help from lovable little Tommy. Do you think I don't know the symptoms of curare poisoning? Whatever you injected into poor Mack had a curare base. Didn't it, Tommy?'

The question came like a whiplash.

'Curare?' echoed Thomson. Deliberately, he spoke loudly. 'I'm not the only one aboard this ship who knows about curare. Or, come to that, who might have used it.'

That comment must have travelled around to Pettigue's ears, as I guessed it was intended to.

'You're a pair of sadistic murderers,' said Lou, with icy distinctness.

Battle was rejoined. I saw I could do nothing to break it up short of turning a fire-hose on them. Maybe they'd quieten down when they'd got it out of their various systems.

Meanwhile, Mack required urgent burial. With repugnance I retrieved him and took him around to the disposal vent on the far side of the ship. Pettigue was standing with one foot on the trap in the floor covering it.

'Pardon me,' I said. He moved aside. This time I saw his eyes. They expressed something at last: sheer flaming murder. But they weren't looking at me. They were staring straight through the huge interposing cone, with its embedded HAPU and solid shields, at the hidden group of quarrellers.

I laid Mack in the small airlock and pressed the button opening its outer door. What Marley pedantically termed the 'angular momentum' of the ship flung Mack off at a tangent into space. It was a path all of our garbage would have to follow.

From a porthole I glimpsed him as a tiny dwindling blot on the Milky Way. Then he was gone. Unlike the dead dog in Verne's moon novel, he wasn't still invisibly bound to the ship and forced to travel alongside it. I felt a twinge of envy. Mack had got clean away to everlasting peace in the wide open spaces.

Leaving me confined with the living wild-cats.

I resolved to spend as little time in their company as possible.

VI

THE TROUBLE WITH MY PLAN TO KEEP MYSELF TO MYSELF was that there was no lock on my door. In fact, there was no door. Anyone could scramble up through the connecting tube.

Exercising my authority, I could have put my cabin out of bounds, even to Marley. I'm not sure why I didn't. Perhaps because the ship was on course, almost everything was automatic, I had too little to do and was bored, and there were three long days to get through before we made the moon.

Only one person could negotiate the connecting tube at a time. Maybe I assumed, therefore, that I'd have only one visitor at a time. Saltpetre, charcoal, and nitre are harmless – separately. Put them together and you have gunpowder. So it was with my crew, I told myself.

What I didn't tell myself was that the only one of them I had any wish to see was Lou. I didn't tell myself because I didn't wish to admit it. Every time I remembered the feel of her body on that beach, every time I heard in my memory her laugh, desire stirred in me. I knew it was dangerous to think about it too much. Does a moth know a flame is dangerous, I wondered?

All I know is I issued no edict to bar the way.

She was the first of them to come. And she came with a scowl.

'One day I'll kill that man stone dead, so help me.'

I didn't ask who. What did it matter? It was an empty threat.

Next minute she was laughing at her own helplessness under free fall. None of them, of course, had experienced the condition before entering my cabin. Dignity is always the first casualty. And you finish up belted in a fixed chair like a victim in a spy thriller.

When Lou was finally secured, she announced: 'I came to make a complaint.'

'About what or who?'

'I can't remember now. It doesn't matter. I'll make another one, instead – against you.'

'Now what have I done?'

'Nothing, Franz. That's just the trouble. You've hidden yourself away in this cabin for hours and hours. You're avoiding me. You're just not giving our love a chance to ripen.'

'It's my cabin. It's my life.'

'This *was* your life, dear man. But you've had it, after this trip. You know that, don't you? Then it'll be, "Home is the sailor, home from space." For good and all. Then what kind of a life will it be, without wife and kids? No life at all. No, you need me, Franz, so stop being evasive.'

'Can you really picture yourself as a mother, Lou?'

She stared at me soberly.

'You seem to have a thing about mothers. A while back you wanted to know what kind of person my mother was. Now you're worried about what kind of a mother I might become. You must have a mother fixation.'

Her stare was penetrating. Whatever the cause, I found myself unable to keep taking it. I looked down at my hands.

'That's scarcely possible, since I never knew my mother. She died in childbirth. I was the child.'

'Do you feel guilty about it?'

'Now, really, Lou—'

'There's no reason for you to feel guilty. You knew nothing. You did nothing. It happened to you, and to your mother, that's all. So don't hang your head, Franz. I know just how you feel.'

I looked at her again. The regard was still searching, but there was tenderness in it now. That was tough to take, too.

She asked: 'Do you ever feel confused, Franz?'

'Sometimes. Like now, for instance.'

'Near our country house there's a big bare hill. Just a clump of trees on the crest, that's all. Like Chanctonbury Ring. There's a terrific view from up there. On a clear day you can see into five counties. I became a pretty confused child, you know, after—'

She broke off, gazing at the chart-screen as though it were displaying something unusual. It wasn't. She'd known how I felt because she had similar moments of irrational self-blame.

Well, I could be blunt, too.

'After your parents were divorced?' I prompted.

'So you know about that. Yes. After that. Sometimes the confusion became so bad it was unbearable. Everything seemed to be in pieces. Everything was meaningless. I kept escaping to that hill. I just wanted to sit on top of it looking down at the world until I could see it whole again. Until all the fields and the lanes and the trees and the villages and the people all came together again and made a picture, some sensible pattern of life. But they wouldn't. I sat there all day many times, in the sun or the rain. And even the trees up there around me didn't seem to form a clump any more. They looked to me like a lot of sulky people who'd quarrelled and turned their backs on each other.'

I nodded, and observed unnecessarily: 'A child tends to personify things.'

'One day I stayed to watch the sunset. Then the stars began to come out and the moon rose like a big golden balloon. I lay watching it, and thinking: maybe people live on the moon. Nice, wise, kind people. Maybe they're looking down at this world, seeing it all in one piece. Not just the fields and woods around me to the edge of the sky, but all over. All over the oceans and Africa and America… Maybe they can even see me and where I fit into it all. One day, I promised myself, I shall go to the moon and ask those wise people: "Where do *I* fit in? You know, don't you? Please tell me."'

I said: 'I wonder if that first put the idea of going to the moon into your head.'

'Perhaps it did. Anyhow, I know I became very interested in astronomy after that. I think I had a lurking hope that somewhere in the universe there was life other and better than mankind. I'd turned away from human-kind. It was mean and petty and dishonest. Greedy and hard and brutal. Nobody gave a damn about anybody but themselves. I desperately needed to believe that there was someone somewhere of real integrity, who you could trust never to let you down.'

She was watching me intently again.

I said, quickly: 'It's obvious why you were hooked by the discovery of those traces of organic life in meteorites. It must have seemed like a kind of promise to you—'

'Promises!' she said, scornfully. 'Only a fool believes a promise is worth anything.'

I shrugged.

She added: 'However, I'm that kind of fool about you, Franz. I'll believe your promises.'

'I haven't made any.'

'You're being very careful not to, aren't you?'

'Admitted.'

'Well, don't be so scared. Nothing you say can make any difference to me now.'

'For this relief, much thanks.'

'I know you, you see, Franz, behind that mask of sarcasm. Ever since that day you first came to our town house, I've known you. I'll always remember the time when my father was explaining this ship to you, but you weren't listening. You were remembering some old tragedy. Your eyes were full of pain. I saw right through them, as though they were windows, into *you*. And I knew right away: this little captain isn't a phony like the others. He's a man, a real man, who *cares*. At last I have found my man. But I have let myself become slack and ugly, because I had given up hope. I disgust him. But now I must pull myself together, make myself worthy of him and win his love. Even if it means following him to the ends of the Earth or to the moon itself. I must never lose him, for he has what I have lost, and he can restore it to me: wholeness, completeness.'

She clasped my wrists with her steady grip.

'Look, there are tears of pain in *my* eyes now, Franz, as there were in yours. Look through them into me. I'm full of love for you. You *must* see it.'

It was like my first encounter with the HAPU again. I didn't want to look, I didn't want to know. Yet I had to, because events were involving me which threatened my future life. I had to face the dangers and size them up.

So I gazed into the dark depths of her eyes. There was love there, all right, of a wild kind. It scared me anew. I had imagined true love was powerful but serene, burning like Pater's 'hard, gemlike flame'. The perfect love that casteth out fear.

Lou's love wasn't like that. It was certainly powerful, but as a thundercloud is powerful. It was full of mad, electric flashes. Plainly, Lou was still a disturbed personality, a kind of human boiling pot of emotions. Fear had not been ousted but remained there in force, with its ugly relatives, hate and despair.

'Lou' was just a collective name for a number of disparate personalities. The cool scientific intelligence dwelt quite apart from the lost, bewildered child. The being who felt tenderly towards me rubbed elbows with one who was arrogantly contemptuous of all men. Among them roved a fury on the loose liable to rend anyone who betrayed, thwarted or slighted her.

All most unsettling.

If I didn't come to terms with this gang, I was in for a bad time. If I did, I should have to live on a knife-edge for evermore.

Lou shifted her hold to the back of my head and pulled my mouth to hers. Her fire poured into me. All critical thought was burned out of me and I was left as mindless as an animal. I seized her and tried to crush her to me, but our respective chair harnesses restrained us and kept our bodies apart. Intense emotion and an element of the ludicrous seem often linked, especially in the sexual act itself.

I heard myself repeating, in something between a murmur and a groan: 'I love you, I love you.'

The thing had happened, and happened of itself.

Later, I reflected that, for good or ill, I was committed now, and Lou's inner conflict was no longer a fight I could honourably stay out of.

The final issue remained in doubt, though. If I were really the integrated character Lou saw me as, I might well pull her through into complete sanity. But I didn't see myself that way at all. I was just a life-long escapist with a hair-trigger temper, sticking my tongue out at authority like a rude schoolboy, concerned about nothing except my individual freedom.

What kind of chance did I stand in this strange spiritual mêlée I'd let myself be sucked into? I could lose this fight. If I did, my own sanity could be lost with it.

At that time of passion, though, all moorings had been swept away. Impulse and suggestion were my masters.

My impatient fingers began to unbuckle Lou's harness.

She whispered: 'My cabin, darling.'

I concurred, for two good reasons. My cabin here was doorless. Hers was not. Her cabin was subjected to artificial gravity. Mine was not. There were difficulties to love-making in a condition of freefall.

For once, I appreciated the benefits of robot control. I had no qualms about quitting my bridge for a while. The ship could govern itself.

Which was more than could be said for its captain.

We went below. The wide ring of the lounge was deserted.

When I came out of Lou's cabin, around an hour later, everyone had taken it into their heads to promenade. Marley and Thomson came along side-by-side discussing deer-stalking – I caught a snatch about 'antler-spread'. Pettigue followed at a distance, almost out of sight up the curve, alone and palely loitering.

Marley suddenly noticed me at Lou's door and stopped dead, with his mouth open. Thomson would never hear the pay-off line of that particular hunting yarn.

The shark's mouth snapped shut. The skin around it went white. This was an unusual colour effect for Marley. Maybe because it was an unusual situation for him. It was for me, too, but I hadn't turned white. I hadn't even turned a hair. Doubtless much of my earlier habitual tension and uncertain temper had arisen simply from corralled energy.

I stayed calm and almost benign.

He came at me like an infuriated rhino. I prepared to sidestep but didn't have to. He burst past me into Lou's cabin.

I looked back and saw her sitting on the bunk drawing a healing zip-tag along the open wound in her natty white suit.

Marley reached back around the door for me, found my arm and pulled it inside. I went along too, as it was obviously going to be painful if I didn't... and perhaps if I did.

He slammed the door shut and bounced me against it a couple of times to prove that he was a bigger man than me. I tried to work up some resentment about this, enough, say, to break his little finger. It was no good. I understood his resentment too well, and forgave him.

Lou said, a bit sharpish, though: 'Careful with that, Dad. It's my property.'

He thrust his face within six inches of mine, glaring. Too close: he tended to squint. He ground out some words slowly but exceeding small: 'This... is... an... outrage.'

'*Was* an outrage,' Lou corrected. 'But I'm not complaining.'

He ignored her.

'I thought I told you to leave my daughter alone.'

'That's odd: I thought you did, too,' I replied, pleasantly. 'And I thought I agreed to.'

'But I thought different,' Lou put in.

'I'll break you for this, Brunel.'

'Can he?' asked Lou.

'Yes,' I said. 'Sub-section Two of Section Twenty-six of the Space Service Rule Book.'

'Never mind, love, I'll support you. I've oodles of money he can't touch.'

Marley spat at her: 'Be quiet. Have you no shame?'

She sat on the bunk, swinging her legs.

'No,' she said. 'Like father, like daughter. You had no shame about going to bed with some women you weren't married to. Even after I was born.'

The silence in the little cabin then was like the moment the bombing stops.

Marley released me. I expected a king-size family row to erupt. But no, the silence went on. Marley clenched and unclenched his hands maybe thrice. He remained pale but a sort of helpless look had replaced the glare. He seemed undecided whether to defend himself, counter-attack, or retreat.

He retreated. He shoved me aside and blundered out.

'There, but for the grace of God, goes a louse,' said Lou.

I said, awkwardly, 'I'd heard he gave your mother a bad time.'

'There you go again. Bring mother into it somehow. Well, she invited her bad time. She was a gentlewoman, you see, not a woman. Too well-bred to lam into him with a rolling-pin until he understood that he was her man alone and not a general bonus issue. She suffered genteelly. You know, pretend nothing's happened so that even your best friends won't tell you that plenty's happened. She pretended so bravely that I didn't know a damn thing was happening. Which made it catastrophic when it all came out with a bang. And came out all wrong. And was never put right.'

'How do you mean, Lou?'

'He framed *her* as the guilty party. My kind, patient mother, who I loved and who I believed loved me, was pilloried as an adulteress. The court confirmed her guilt, and I had been brought up to believe the law was never wrong. So I stayed with my father, who I also loved and who I believed loved me. And tried to forget my gentle hypocrite of a mother who had betrayed him. So she went away and quietly died somewhere, as women of that kind will themselves to do when they're deprived of all affection. When it was too late, I found out the real truth. She died unconsoled, and remains unavenged – except in such petty measure as I've succeeded in giving my father hell.'

I went and took her in my arms. I felt big and manly and protective, even though I wasn't big and uncharitably could be compared to a Scotch terrier guarding its mistress.

However, we found comfort in each other, and that was a big thing to me. On this same bunk I'd lost many of those old doubts about Franz Brunel, Captain, Space Service, his worth and significance – together with much of his egotism, irritability, and irresponsibility. I really believed Lou and I would make out, somehow, whatever the world had done to us.

Unfortunately, the past isn't discarded quite so easily and finally as that.

At last I decided I ought to pay some attention to my other duty, the one I received pay for. I gave Lou one more kiss, then started back to my control cabin. And walked into more trouble en route.

Marley's thwarted anger with Lou and me had found an alternative target: that born scapegoat, Pettigue. I was just in time to see him push Pettigue so hard in the chest that the little chap sprawled half on his back on the curved lounge couch. Marley stood over him, bellowing and waving a book threateningly.

I went up to them, and asked coldly: 'What's going on?'

'Never you mind,' Marley said, roughly, not even turning.

For all his bulk, in my eyes, in my mood, he looked pretty small. Marley, I said silently, you're *nothing*.

Aloud, I said: 'Still shoving the little boys in the playground around, Marley? But you've left school now. I won't tolerate bullying on my ship.'

'So?'

'So you'll apologize to Mr Pettigue.'

Pettigue muttered: 'I want no part of him, certainly not his spurious apologies.'

'Look, *Captain* Brunel,' said Marley, heavily, 'I start nothing unless provoked, and if you don't call this provocation, then I do.'

He exhibited the book. It was the book of books to him, and he carried it around like a personal bible: Robert W. Service's *The Trail of '98*.

'I'd been reading this. I left it open on that seat. When I came back for it, it was shut. When I opened it…'

He opened it. A big, damp, grey blob of chewing gum was stuck between the pages, one of which had been torn right across – doubtless by his own inadvertent act.

Marley went on: 'There's only one person aboard who chews this disgusting stuff, despite that I ordered him not to.'

I looked inquiringly at Pettigue.

He said, faintly: 'I know nothing about it, Captain. I've not used gum since blast-off.'

'Certainly I've not seen you do so,' I said.

'Unless you've been following him around, that means nothing,' said Marley.

I said: 'Let's try to keep a sense of proportion – this isn't a murder investigation. Personally, I believe Pettigue simply because he's not the type—'

'Pettigue isn't a type,' Marley interrupted. 'Whatever he is, he isn't that. You don't know much about him, obviously.'

Which was roughly true.

'All right. I regret the damage to your book. But does it matter so terribly?'

'It matters to me. This is a scarce first edition of what I consider to be the greatest adventure saga ever written. I've treasured it since I was a young man. And now this fool has ruined it. I could break his neck.'

Pettigue muttered something under his breath.

I said: 'I still don't think he did it. I know *I* didn't – I have an alibi.' I couldn't resist that dig at him. 'Which leaves only your pal, Tommy the jester. This is the kind of nasty little joke he'd go for, knowing that Pettigue would get the blame: that makes it all the more hilarious.'

Marley stared at me.

'Tommy wouldn't do a mean thing like this to me.'

'Tommy would. Tommy likes to make trouble for people, and especially for Pettigue.'

Marley pondered. He'd known Thomson a darn sight longer than I had, so it was unlikely that he was unaware of his infantile quirks. Abruptly, he strode off towards Thomson's cabin.

Pettigue sighed, then murmured: 'Thanks, Captain.'

I said: 'Thomson will deny it, of course, and then they may both be after your hide. You'd better keep out of the way for a bit. I'm just going aloft. Why not tag along?'

'Thanks again.'

I had a few things to do in my eyrie, communication-wise mainly, and left Pettigue to his own devices, which were limited by the chair straps. So he watched me.

When I'd finished, he remarked: 'I can see why they picked you for pilot. You handle everything so efficiently.'

'Don't let mere briskness fool you, Pet. I *am* efficient, granted, but here there's little call to be. The ship practically handles itself. Anyone who can press a button could call himself its pilot. You could, for instance.'

I was playing it down, rather. The lunar landing still loomed ahead as a real test of my efficiency. It had to be done by the chemical rockets. If there *were* any kind of micro-life on the moon, you could hardly expect to find it still extant in an area you'd just blasted with radio-active gas.

However, I was worrying less now. Nothing boosts a man's morale so much as the discovery that he loves and is loved in return. He feels equal to almost anything.

'I wonder,' speculated Pettigue, 'if I really could.'

His washed-out eyes had a rare gleam of excitement in them.

Poor little guy, I thought, with his built-in inferiority complex and habit of sad comparisons. His morale could use a boost, too. To believe he could put the *Endeavour* through its paces, if called upon, might make him feel one up on his boss and persecutor. Anyhow, it would pass the time for both of us while he was hiding out here...

'You've got it, Pet: that's all there is to it,' I said, after a half-hour of instruction. 'All you need to do now is mail off an application for your pilot's badge.'

Wonder of wonders, he smiled. It was more of a rictus, but at least something had amused him.

'Thank you, Captain,' he said, quietly.

Now I wished to be quit of him. No reflection on him – he'd been surprisingly quick on the uptake, a good pupil. But every minute away from Lou intensified my urge to be with her again. Her image kept interposing itself between me and everything I tried to do.

I said: 'It sounds all quiet below, so maybe the storm's blown itself out now.'

He took the hint and began to unfasten his harness.

'Absurd, isn't it?' he said. 'All that uproar over a piece of chewing gum.'

'The War of Jenkins's Ear was absurd, too, but it happened.'

He nodded, and said slowly: 'Yes. These crazy things do happen.'

Just as slowly, he disappeared down the connecting tube.

I waited a while, hoping Lou would call me or call on me. A childish misgiving began to nag: maybe she doesn't need me around as badly as I need her.

At last, I reached for the intercom phone. As I grasped it, I heard someone begin to work their way up through the connecting tube. I watched the aperture eagerly.

Disappointment: it was only her father.

A changed Marley, though, from his last aspect. He was discharging cordiality from every pore, but I suspected the pumps were primed. Affability in a person like Marley was apt to breed suspicion in a person like me.

He had the usual stock-in-trade of the professional politician, though I'll allow he eschewed the more patent gimmicks – the permanent cigar, the exaggerated quiff or outlandish hat – which makes it so easy to confuse a Home Secretary with a classic Mack Sennett film comedian.

Instead, he banked on personality gimmicks. Instant charm. The level gaze intended to demonstrate he was levelling with you.

The friendly hand laid lightly on your shoulder, poised to break into its routine of encouraging pats.

As he approached me now, shifting awkwardly between hand and footholds, he yet contrived to keep all gimmicks cocked for action. So I knew he wanted something from me, and wondered what I had that could be of any possible value to him.

'How many knots have we pegged today, Captain?'

Affability had been injected into his tone like cream into a cream puff. (Too bad that cream puffs make me bilious.)

I gave him the day's mileage in round figures.

'Which puts us here,' he said, tapping a finger on the ground glass of the orbit chart. He knew where to tap it. A tiny spot of light, imperceptibly moving, marked our position. I suppose he was accustomed to sycophants who'd react to this pointless performance as though it were a demonstration of mathematical genius.

'That's what the computer says.'

'H'm.'

My tactless response didn't deflate him. He wriggled into the opposite chair, and came at me from another angle: the strictly-between-ourselves one.

'Strictly between ourselves, Tommy can be a bit of a stinker sometimes.'

'That's strictly between everyone who's ever met him.'

'He said he knew nothing about that gum business. But I could see he was lying. You don't reach my station in life without the ability to size up a man.'

'I never heard that you objected to a fool and a liar marrying your daughter.'

This, normally, would have caused him to burst his chair straps. He just breathed a little more deeply and kept his mask on.

'Don't misunderstand me, Captain. Tommy has many good qualities. But we all have our little failings—'

'He's a drunk, too,' I said, crudely.

He gestured deprecatingly, and switched on to his real aim.

'We're nearing the critical point on the orbital path, Captain, and it's my duty to hand you these sealed orders.'

He produced an envelope red-splashed with sealing wax and pushed it at me.

'What the hell is this?' I growled. 'I wasn't told about any sealed orders.'

I read the envelope's contents with amazed anger. There was a covering note of authority signed by the Minister for Spatial Research, who was an accredited fool named Charleston, an admirer and crony of Marley's.

I was directed to alter course and make for a totally different landing area, which was specified.

So there was yet another unadmitted reason for carrying a pilot experienced in manual control. I'd been kept in the dark by people planning to use me.

The reborn Franz Brunel, self-possessed man of the world, was overcome by the old fury, the black hatred of any *sub rosa* hanky-panky.

I exploded.

'This is rank lunacy! Don't deny it, Marley: you're behind this. I don't know how you talked this clot Charleston into it, but you're both out of your minds. It's sabotage. More than that – it's murder. And, just as a side-issue, it's a unilateral revocation of the Lunar Territorial Agreement. Does the Prime Minister know about this?'

Marley was gripping and twisting his chair-arms so fiercely that the torque produced a squeak.

'The P.M. trusts his Ministers,' he said, stiff-faced.

'You mean he knows – unofficially – but he'll deny it if there's a loud enough squawk. God, you political schemers make me sick to my stomach. Well, you can all go take a running jump. I'm responsible for the safety of my ship and all aboard her. I alone. If I were fool enough to try to set her down in that mess of rock piles, I'd smash her to pieces. Every space-ship landing is a kind of controlled crash, tough enough to pull off even when the surface is flat as a lawn. So why pick just about the worst landing spot on the moon? What's the big idea of this switch, anyhow?'

The original landing site given to me was on the Mare Nubium, a fine smooth place. The new order was to land at a point a little to the east of Tycho among a tight-packed jumble of small inter-locking craters.

Marley hedged. 'You're scared to put her down there, Captain?'

'I'd be a nut if I wasn't. Nobody can land a ship on a moun-tainside. The only flat area in those parts is inside Tycho itself.'

'No, that won't do. Tycho's walls are twelve thousand feet high. We'd waste days climbing out, if we ever got out. Tycho's rays don't originate in the crater but at a point outside it.'

'What the devil have Tycho's rays to do with it?'

'Why don't you simply obey orders without question, Captain?'

'Orders to commit suicide? No, I'm just an old-fashioned democrat. I like to know what I'm dying for.'

Marley rubbed his nose thoughtfully.

Then: 'All right, you'll have to know sooner or later, anyway. Now, as you're aware, that huge territory which includes Tycho and its strange, bright radial streaks is still unallocated, no-man's-land.'

'Sure. And, as you're aware, while the dispute continues it would be a breach of the Agreement to set foot in it.'

'Precisely: it remains unexplored – that's the point.'

'Except from space itself,' I said.

'Yes, but that's not the same as being on the spot. It leaves a lot to guesswork. Like the constitution of those streaks, or rays, for instance. Well, here's news for you! Our boys in the space-station recently completed an observational test on them with a new gadget which uses polarized light. The rays are definitely metallic.'

'Hardly news,' I said. 'The old volcanic ash theory went out of the window even before anyone reached the moon. Most everyone agreed they were metal.'

'Oh, yes, but what *kind* of metal? This gadget indicated it's almost certainly gold.'

One clean four-letter word, and all was explained. It was the keyword to the mystery of the change of plan.

'You really *were* bitten by that gold-bug, weren't you, Marley?'

'I never pretended I wasn't. Those streaks add up to countless square miles of open goldfields. The biggest bonanza ever, and I'm going to make it.'

The chair-arms began to squeak again. He was rocking with excitement.

He needed cooling off with a splash of cold water.

So I said: 'First, it may not be gold at all – merely pyrites. Second, I won't attempt to land at that spot for all the gold on the moon or anywhere else. If I tried to, you wouldn't survive to make your strike, I can assure you. And I don't give a damn about a court martial, excommunication, or being shot at dawn. The P.M. wouldn't dare. I'm observing international law. He isn't.'

Marley froze. This was the ultimate frustration. His basilisk stare had cold murder in it.

After a silence, he said: 'All right, Brunel, maybe I can't nail you for that. But I can for the most serious crime in the Rule Book. You know what I mean.'

'Yes. Sub-section Two of Section Twenty-six.'

'Now, listen, Captain. I'll withdraw that charge on condition you comply with those written orders. Moreover, I'll not stand in the way of your marrying Lou, if that's what you want.'

'So you'd barter even your only daughter for gold, eh?'

A silly crack of mine in response to a silly remark of his. Lou was well above the age of consent. He brushed it aside.

'Well, Brunel?'

'Wait a minute. Let me think about it.'

It was true that he could get me dismissed with ignominy, and probable loss of pension, for flagrant violation of both the rules and Lou. However, I was no respecter of rules. If I had to pay the price, then I'd pay it. It was a high price: space travel had been my whole life. But it wasn't any more. If I had to choose between it and Lou, I'd choose Lou.

On the other hand, I wasn't overmuch worried about violating the Lunar Territorial Agreement, either. In a way, the duplicity of the P.M. was comparable to that of Queen Elizabeth I, who privately encouraged Drake to trespass in Spanish colonies and loot them of gold and publicly washed her hands of him.

And I also recalled Lord Nelson turning a blind eye on occasion.

The dispute over the lunar no-man's-land had dragged on for years, squalidly. Nobody would give an inch, and everybody imagined therefore they were being tough. In fact, they were merely being greedy, mulish, and mean-spirited.

If some neo-Elizabethan freebooters lost patience and acted where these space lawyers only argued interminably, I should be with them in spirit. So why shouldn't I be with them in fact?

I never bucked risks that were worth it. Was this one worth it?

I said: 'Gold is where you find it, as I told you once before. But where you find it is directly related to its value. You've got to reckon the transport costs. Gold on Earth is valuable most anywhere. But gold on the moon...? It's heavy stuff. I know that eventually this atomic drive is bound to cheapen transport per pound of payload. But will it reach the degree of becoming worth its weight in gold, so to speak? You know what it's cost to get the *Endeavour* off the ground—'

'The *Endeavour* is a passenger ship,' broke in Marley. 'Passenger transport is always far costlier than pure freight. The gold can be shot back to Earth in one-way, unmanned freight rockets. An American named Hugo Gernsback worked out the details many years ago. He had a record of accurate prophecy of scientific inventions comparable to that of H. G. Wells. Somewhere at home I've the plans of a space-suit, not so very different from the type we're carrying, he published way back in 1919.'

Characteristically, Marley had the facts and figures in his memory, and gave me an economic break-down of the simple beryllium radio-guided freight-sphere Gernsback had designed on paper. It would be expelled from an atomic launcher mounted on the moon, and carry nothing but its retro-rockets, radio gear, and cargo of gold. Its weight on the moon would be but one-sixth of its Earth weight, and would take correspondingly less power to launch.

It would fall, radio-guided, into the sea and float. The beryllium could be melted down and its cost recovered.

I considered the proposition, and sold myself on it.

'All right, Marley. It's feasible. But it's still not feasible to land anywhere near the focal point of Tycho's rays. The terrain is impossible, believe me. But we could land on another part of the Mare Nubium where one of the major rays crosses it. Near enough to it for you to reach it. We'll be on the wrong side of the frontier, but only just. We might get away with the plea of a navigational mistake over the Mare. I should have to take the rap for that, of course. But I think, somehow, the P.M. will see to it that I remain in the Service.'

Marley relaxed with a long sigh.

'That's reasonable. I'll go along with that. You're an awkward customer but you do have some sense and spirit. You might make a tolerable son-in-law at that, Brunel.'

'Call me Franz,' I said, winningly.

VII

At 15.45 G.M.T. on June 21st the *ENDEAVOUR* made a perfect landing on the Mare Nubium.

For an authoritative description, see page 112 of *Conquest of the Moon*, by W. L. Burton, who wasn't there, of course. But I gave him the facts. Most of them, anyhow.

I reserved the one that somehow I missed firing chemical tank Three at the correct time, and if the gyroscopes hadn't been as good as they were could easily have made a disastrous approach at some 30 degrees from the vertical.

However, despite the gyros straining their guts to compensate for my error – or maybe because of it – I sensed something wasn't right, checked, and threw the switch in time to avert calamity.

I was alone in the control cabin and so was the sole witness of my bath of cold sweat.

This, I told myself, is what comes of succumbing to the habit of leaving it to the robots. The rot had set in during a mere three days. Slackness. Rust-spots on the memory. This was what automation was doing to people on Earth. It was a poor look-out for everyone.

Well, maybe that was part of it. But infatuation with Lou did nothing to help me to concentrate on my work.

What a fool time to fall in love, I thought.

She had the commonsense to stay away from me during the tricky stages, but I hadn't the sense to put her out of my mind.

However, she turned up at my side two minutes after touch-down and congratulated me with a hug and the verdict: 'A peach, Franz – we landed like a bit of thistle-down.'

Bill Burton, in his book, praised the masterly landing, too, but spoiled the effect rather by adding that I had mistaken the map reference. That I'd touched down twenty miles from Bullialdus instead of the same distance from Copernicus, with which I had confused it. He was tactful about it, and pointed out that these two craters were easy to confuse, being of the same type, sizeable, and with terraced ramparts.

Moreover, he added, the light was poor. Because of the danger of solar flares (high-energy protons spewed out intermittently by the sun) the landing had to be made on the night side of the moon, so that the moon itself would shield us from them.

In fact, the light was good. It was Earthlight, and that's plenty to see your way around by. Earth's albedo is point four, which means that it reflects two-fifths of the sunlight which falls on it.

And when the wind is southerly I know Copernicus from Bullialdus. It was a deliberate mistake. I was keeping both faith with Marley and a plausible out for when the international rumpus started.

There was a crate of champagne aboard for the celebration of this moment, but only Dr Thomson did justice to it. I had a few sips from Lou's glass, having no time for more because the radio demanded all of my attention. For once, Marley left me to it. I was stuck with a continent-wide hook-up agog for my on-the-spot reports. Also, every big bug connected with the Project was scrambling to get in with his ten cents' worth of congratulation.

I accepted on behalf of my crew, and on behalf of Marley, whom they kept clamouring for. But he was too pre-occupied with scrambling himself – into his space-suit. He was swearing steadily at recalcitrant fastenings.

He knew he was within walking distance of his big strike, at last. He was mad with impatience and nothing else mattered.

The nearer edge of the ray lay around five miles from the ship. He kept pausing to peer out of a port in that direction hoping to glimpse it. I told him twice it was out of sight over the horizon, which, of course, is much nearer on the moon than on Earth. Then I shut up, because reason couldn't touch his gold-obsessed mind.

Pettigue was also putting on his suit, but carefully and slowly, as though he were reluctant to. I guessed he was. Tough as the material was, it wasn't impervious to micro-meteorites. On Earth, the atmosphere saves us from them: it burns them up through friction. On the moon, only one thing could save you: luck. You had to hold on to the hope that there wasn't a micro-meteorite with your name on it. Nature was sniping at you out there.

The chances of being hit were far higher than being struck by lightning back home, yet not necessarily so lethal. If only your suit were holed, but not you, the moon's vacuum would suck eagerly at the air in your suit and try to suffocate you. However, such a danger had long been foreseen, and there was an emergency drill for it.

All the same, you were under fire, and I could see that Pettigue wasn't looking forward to his baptism.

Marley suddenly noticed Lou pouring a second glass of champagne.

'That's enough, Lou,' he said, sharply. 'Why aren't you getting into your suit?'

'I'm waiting for Franz.'

'There's no need for you to wait for him. They won't let him leave the transmitter for a long time yet. I thought you'd at least be interested in getting out to check up on your theories.'

'Of course, Dad. But if there's life out there, it's been there for a million years, maybe. It can wait for another hour.'

I turned from the set long enough to say: 'It would pay you to be patient, too, Marley. The four of you could unload and assemble the runabout in a couple of hours. It would save you a long walk, and you wouldn't lose a lot of time.'

'I don't want to lose *any* time,' said Marley, tersely. 'I've waited all my life to strike gold. I can't stay fooling around here now.'

I shrugged and turned back.

Then Marley said, in a different tone, near to pleading: 'Get into your suit, Lou. I'd like you to be with me when I make the strike.'

I expected her to give him the brush-off with some crack or other.

Instead of which, she said, quietly: 'Okay, Dad.'

I had what I thought was a private moment of chagrin, but Thomson, straightening up from the crate with another bottle in his hand, caught my expression and smiled unsympathetically.

I scowled at him, and said, evenly: 'Thank you, Sir Robert. We're all as happy as you are about it, I can assure you.'

Sir Robert Maine, top atomic physicist in the Project, sitting comfortably in his office in distant Harwell, had a postscript: 'Doctor Zignawitsch also wishes to add his congratulations.'

'I'm honoured,' I said, trying not to make it sound sarcastic.

Then I snatched a moment to tell Thomson: 'Help Lou on with her suit.'

'Never mind, Tommy,' said Lou. 'I can manage.'

Thomson smiled crookedly, levelled the bottle at her as if it were a gun and started to untwist the wire holding the cork. At the last moment, he righted the bottle and the cork hit the ceiling.

He poured the foaming stuff into his glass and said to me: 'Lou doesn't like me to touch her. Not any more.'

I was annoyed, as he intended, by the implication that there was a time when she did like him to.

I snapped: 'All right, but you can still do something more useful than emptying those bottles. Get the suit sets tested and netted.'

Each space-suit had a small built-in receiver/transmitter through which the wearer maintained a link with the other suited personnel. Before anyone left the ship, their set had to be tuned, or netted, to a further two-way radio in my control cabin.

I left him to get on with it, for the Earth-moon link drew me into it again. This time it was the Prime Minister himself. He had once been a pilot, too, although solely of aircraft, and remained keen, technically-minded and inquisitive.

His drumfire questions taxed my knowledge, wits, and stamina. They went on and on.

At long last: 'Well, thank you very much, Captain Brunel, for being so patient with me and for supplying so much valuable gen. We Earthbound specimens here won't take up any more of your time now, as you must be bursting to get cracking on a spot of exploration. Contact us again in your own good time. We'll be all ears, you can be sure.'

Yes, I thought, you old fox. You'll be all ears to learn whether thar's gold in them thar rays.

Aloud, I said: 'Thank you, Sir. Goodbye for now. Off.'

My mouth was dry with talking, and I could use my belated drink. I reached for an empty glass, then for a bottle, which proved to be equally empty.

Only Thomson was left in the cabin with me. He lay in a chair, so relaxed he appeared boneless. His eyes had a bright glaze. In an unfocused way he watched me picking up and putting down bottles without getting anywhere.

''Fraid you're too late for the party, old man,' he said, thickly. 'The bubbly's all gone. Mostly inside little me. The others weren't really interested, silly people.'

'Thanks very much,' I said, bitingly.

'Don't snarl at me, old man. Don't take it out on me just 'cos Lou went off with Daddy and didn't wait for you.'

Yet another opportunity to practise self-restraint. I practised hard.

'Where are they now?' I asked, restrainedly.

He tapped the radio beside him. It was humming with etheric noise.

'Ask 'em.'

I flipped the 'Send' switch.

'Captain calling. Report, Colonel Marley.'

A louder hum from the speaker and a bass voice sang through it: *'I'm off for Californy with my washbowl on my knee...'*

It wasn't easy to picture Marley as a songster, but it was his voice, sure enough. For once, he sounded like a happy man. The song, of course, was a favourite of the old 'Forty-Niners', a variant on *Oh, Susannah*.

He broke off, and said: 'Marley. We're making good progress. Bounding along. It's all hop, skip and jump – as easy as pie. Have you tried it yet, Captain? Over.'

'No, I haven't. Have you set up an ARU yet?'

ARU: Automatic Relay Unit. The moon has no Heaviside Layer canopying it to reflect radio waves and bounce them over its surface. When you journeyed beyond the transmitter's horizon, the waves couldn't pursue your descending course. So you deposited a portable ARU at a strategic point to keep you in touch with the base transmitter as far as the next horizon.

That is, if you remembered to take one with you. Marley had been in too much haste to think of it. However, instead of blaming someone else, he apologized. Definitely, he was in an unprecedented state of good humour.

I asked Lou: 'How come *you* overlooked it?'

She sounded light-hearted, too.

'Had an attack of love-sickness. Still suffering from it. What would you prescribe, Captain?'

'I'm not prepared to tell you in public. Go carefully, dear. Don't fall down any crevices beyond the horizon, for, remember, we shan't be able to hear any SOS calls. I'll get the runabout ready just as soon as I can, and come after you.'

'Okay, darling. It's pretty marvellous out here. I can see…'

She faded out quite rapidly. I called her again, and Marley also. No reply. They had passed the last possible point of communication.

Another voice came on the net, after a respectful wait. 'Pettigue calling, Captain. I'm about a mile from the ship, due west, collecting mineral specimens. The going is easy and the suit is functioning well. Do you have any specific orders? Over.'

I hesitated a few moments, weighing up Thomson. I needed help with the runabout. I decided that Thomson, in his present condition, would be useless. Worse than that: dangerous. A monster waited outside the ship, ready to pounce if any of us intruders from another world put a foot wrong.

A monster composed of – nothing. In its very nothingness lay its power to kill.

The space-suits weren't completely foolproof, neither were the *Endeavour's* airlocks. Forget to turn one switch, or even turn one at the wrong time, and the monster could suck ferociously until you were dead.

I depressed the 'Send' switch and answered: 'Yes, Pettigue, come in now. I need your assistance here.'

Then I rounded on Thomson. 'Drunkenness on duty. You know I'm bound to report this?'

'Report away. What the hell do I care?'

'That's the root of the trouble. You never have cared about anyone but yourself.'

Thomson foolishly wagged a finger. 'Now you're preaching at me just like Lou used to do. 'Course, she never practised what she preached. Preachers never do. Lou cares about just one little thing: to get what she wants. To do that she'll bully, sulk, lie or scheme. And, if driven to it, she'd go further than that, Franzy – she'd kill. She once damn near killed her old man. And she's been killing me for years… slowly.'

I got some soluble tablets from the medicine chest and stirred three of them in a tumbler of water.

'Drink that. It'll help sober up your nasty little mind.'

He tossed down the potion as though it were another scotch.

Presently, he said: 'My mother was "fey", you know. Primitive Scottish term meaning the possession of pre-psycho para-cognition.'

'You mean para-psychological precognition?'

'Um – yes. Lord, you're right. I *am* tight. Funny thing – sometimes when I'm tight like this the old fey streak comes out in me too. I've got it now. And it tells me this, Brunel: death is near. Yes, death. Mine, yours, whose – I dunno. So watch out.'

There was a sudden solemnity in his drink-blurred voice.

'Watch out,' he repeated. 'Trust nobody, not even yourself. And never, *never* trust that horrid little man you've just been speaking to. Dear little Pet! For my money, a homicidal maniac and mass murderer.'

'Stand up,' I said.

'What?'

'Stand up. That's it. Now let go of the chair. Okay? Right. Start walking around slowly and keep going. You're going to walk yourself sober.'

He looked at me with red eyes, and for a moment I thought I would have to twist his arm.

Then he slurred: 'To hear is to obey, O Master.'

He began to stagger around the perimeter of the cabin, pausing now and then to steady himself against the wall.

'All right, don't believe me,' he said. 'But look up Pet's record sometime. Tough little bastard. He survives all the expeditions – alone. There was the Alaskan expedition. Wiped out by an avalanche. Except Pettigue. He came back to tell the tale. Then there was the Mato Grosso affair. It so happens I know something special about that.'

It so happened that I did also. I was curious to know if it was the same thing: Pettigue's abandonment of his colleagues. I let Thomson ramble on, as he continued to circle the cabin.

'I don't have many friends. Not at the same time, anyhow. They come, they go. People seem to like me at first. And then… they drift away. Guess my cynicism gets 'em down in the end. But I still have one pal who's stuck with me since we were at medical college. Pete Thorneycroft. He was the medico on the trip into the Mato Grosso. There were exactly two survivors: Pete and Pet. Pete, because he'd picked up swamp fever and was sent back. Pettigue, because – well, who knows?'

'They were attacked by Indians. He was lucky enough to escape. What's the mystery?' I said.

'How were they killed, Franz?'

'Arrows, I heard.'

'Arrows. Poisoned arrows.' He chuckled. 'Poisoned with curare, of course, in those parts. Funny: Lou accused me of killing her cat with curare.'

'What's funny about it?'

'Oh, I don't know. There's more than one way to kill a cat... with curare. You don't need an arrow to get it into the blood-stream. You know, Pete Thorneycroft told me there was just one tribe of Indians in that neck of the woods where it happened. And they used blowpipes, not bows. Darts, not arrows. The nearest forest archers live some two hundred miles to the north of that area.'

'Thorneycroft could have been mistaken. Or, in the confusion, Pettigue could have been mistaken.'

'He mistook darts for arrows?'

'Hell, it's possible,' I said, irritably. 'I doubt if he had time to stand around taking notes.'

'No, maybe not. I wonder why the Indians let him get away?'

'Drop it, Tommy. It's over and done with.'

'Is it?' he muttered, as he passed me on another wavering circuit. 'Is it?'

Then it was that I noticed the radio 'Send' switch was still depressed. With a stab of guilt over my carelessness, I flipped it up. Thomson didn't see: his back was towards me.

The live mike must have picked up much of our talk. Marley and Lou were out of range. But Pettigue wasn't.

Proverbially, listeners seldom hear good of themselves.

I felt a fit of the blues coming on, generated by diverse misgivings.

About Pettigue and his reaction to these slanderous imputations.

About myself and my second boob over switch procedure. (A robot which failed twice thus would be scrapped.)

About Lou: beyond reach, in more senses than one. I was beginning to despair that I should ever really understand her. I knew a little of her complex and contradictory nature, but there was so much more I didn't know. And I had always assumed that perfect understanding was necessary for perfect love. Maybe I assumed too much.

Be that as it may, I cared about what might be happening out there over the horizon's rim. The meteoric hazard was real, but I was more afraid of Marley's impetuosity. He'd already led her into taking a foolish risk, and as they neared the maybe golden ray, he was bound to become ever more excited and heedless.

Gloomily, I watched Thomson on his rounds and reflected that, self-centred though he was, it was probable he knew a deal more about Lou than I did.

At last he mumbled 'That's enough,' and flopped back into his chair.

He glanced at me and said sarcastically: 'The Leith polithe dishmisses me, three times. Satisfied, Captain, or do you insist on a blood test?'

I let it pass, and ventured: 'In your capacity as the family doctor, did you attempt any psychiatric treatment with Lou? I know you're a qualified—'

'You should also know it would be a breach of medical ethics for me to disclose anything about it,' he cut in, still sardonic.

'All right. Forget it.'

'If you want to know why she skipped off hand in hand with Daddy, it's because she loves him. Or why she once nearly killed him, and may yet kill him, it's because she hates him. The old man feels much the same way about her, too. It's a classic mutual love-hate relationship. And if you're fool enough to marry her, the pattern will repeat itself with you. I know. I've had some. She can't help herself. That pattern was burned into her nervous system. She projects it unconsciously upon every close relationship. Love and hate are as inseparable to her as the two sides of a coin. Take her love, if you must – but remember, you have to accept the other side of the coin, too.'

'Thanks,' I said, dubiously.

He laughed. 'Why the hell should I warn you? Nobody warned me.'

'Maybe you're just trying to warn me off. You're still in love with her yourself, aren't you? Maybe you want her back.'

'Yes, old boy, I want her back. What was that little piece Bill Blake wrote about life being joy and woe woven fine? It's true, anyhow. You've got to accept life on those terms. If you don't you'll never know what life really is. To me, Lou is life itself. I don't reject her: she rejects me. So I turn to the bottle for a companion instead. It makes slow death a little easier to endure.'

For the first time, I came near to feeling sorry for the man. In his own way he was as lonely and frustrated as Pettigue.

Which reminded me that Pettigue should be returning at any moment now. And that we had a job to get on with: we hadn't come a quarter of a million miles merely to sit around discussing our personal problems.

I said: 'Yes, life can be tough. However, before you expire finally, come down and help with the runabout.'

Thomson registered my change of tone, gave a little shrug, and said: 'Aye, aye, sir.'

In the early stages it was assumed that the runabout would be stowed aboard in full running order. Thus, after the landing, we could bundle into it as it stood in its airlock, bowl down a ramp, and go sailing off over the bounding *Mare*.

When the ship was half built, the design engineers discovered, in that cute way they have, that some of their calculations were straight fantasy. The ship was just that dangerous bit short on chemical drive. An additional fuel tank needed to be fitted into the space which they hadn't allowed for it.

So they stole the space from the runabout's garage and stuck the tank there.

Their argument: the fuel in it would be used up during the landing operation. So, afterwards, the tank could be jettisoned, leaving the garage wholly free again. Fair enough, but until that moment the diminished garage space would be insufficient to accommodate the runabout.

Adaptable as chameleons, they came out in favour of reducing the runabout to a small, one-man vehicle.

They were surprised and injured when I made a stand against that. It would mean, I said, that three-quarters of the party would be permanently anchored in the vicinity of the ship. Our time on the moon was limited. Every minute of it should be used in exploration. Restricted mobility would criminally waste time.

However, they became reasonable and co-operative about it – after I'd threatened to go to the P.M. in person. (Idle threat: I knew that my chances of reaching him, if doubled or trebled, still amounted to nil.) They tried to find a way of packing the runabout in parts for quick and easy assembly. It was still an impossibly tight squeeze.

I asked to see the plans, and was allowed to, for the first time.

One of the problems, volume wise, was a bristling array of long jointed arms bearing rows of wide plates.

'What the hell are those for?' I inquired. 'To guard against the bites of sharks?'

It was a would-be comic reference to the White Knight's useless impedimenta, and was lost on them. For they were quite as crazy as the White Knight himself. They informed me gravely that these were solar batteries to supplement the main battery.

Solar batteries operate, of course, by gathering sunlight.

I asked them how we should be able to gather sunlight on the night side of the moon, which was all that we were scheduled to see. It was almost unbelievable, but they hadn't known that.

Compartmentalization is the curse of all top secret construction jobs. You keep happening upon such pockets of engineers, with no clear picture of the overall plan, sweating away on futile work.

When they'd scrapped the battery arms it was easy to store the runabout. In thirty-two pieces... But it wasn't all that easy to re-assemble those pieces. On trial runs we learned that an octopus might manage it, but one man was limited by having only two hands. Four hands were the minimum. Six were better still.

Thomson's hands were still shaky but I should have to make do with them. I took them all the way down to the garage. Thomson perforce came with them, but that's life: you can't have it all ways.

We detached the pipes from the empty tank and retired to an ante-chamber. The garage space was designed to become an airlock in itself.

Watching through an observation port, I pressed a stud. The outer wall of the garage swung open like a door. A section of the floor slid out through the aperture, like a protruding tongue. It bore, balanced on it, the big cylindrical tank, rocking slightly in the gale of released air. The tongue extended to its full length and stopped.

I pressed the multi-purpose stud again. The tongue tilted downward, became a wide ramp. The cylinder rolled down it and trundled on across the lunar surface. Just before it disappeared from my limited view I glimpsed a small space-suited figure hop like a flea out of its path.

The moon endowed all Earthlings, including even Pettigue, with the elevation and slow grace of a Nijinski.

I chuckled.

Thomson asked: 'What's funny?'

'Pettigue was just outside the door. The tank darn near steam-rollered him.'

'It would have been a lot funnier if it had have done.'

I ignored the typical sneer and waited for Pettigue. Presently, he came trudging up the ramp, trailing a container presumably full of mineral specimens. When he was safely inside, I hit the stud again. The ramp rose to the horizontal and hung there. Another jab, and it began to withdraw into the ship. Pettigue stood aside and let it re-occupy its groove.

I started the airlock cycling. Then, when the air pressure evened, I moved back into the garage and helped the little man remove his helmet.

'What's it like out there, Pet?'

Looking at the general area of my navel, he muttered: 'It's all right.'

Thomson, behind me, commented: 'You don't sound exactly over-enthusiastic.'

Pettigue turned his back on him and began to open his specimen container.

'Leave that – it can wait,' I told him. 'Just get your suit off. And, Tommy, start unpacking the runabout.'

I joined him at the task. The protective packing was tough, and I tore a fingernail ripping it from the part I awarded priority. This was the dashboard with fitted radio. I tuned the instrument and called the Marleys. No response. I supposed they were still messing around somewhere beyond the skyline. I left it at 'Receive'.

And that reminded me that Pettigue must have done some involuntary receiving.

I glanced at him to check if he were registering suppressed anger. He was taut and suppressing some emotion, obviously, but it seemed to me more fear than anger.

I said, at a venture: 'Pet, you weren't happy out there, were you?'

He shook his head and said, tight-lipped: 'The eternal silence of these infinite spaces frightens me.'

One of Pascal's better-known *Pensées*.

Thomson looked up from the huge wheel he was uncovering and quipped sarcastically: 'To be frightened of nothing means that you must be a brave little man.'

'Nothing can be pretty frightening if you step on it, thinking that something's there,' I said.

'If space scares him, then he was a damn fool to come,' said Thomson. 'Space is no place for anyone with agoraphobia.'

'But he came,' I said. 'Was that foolishness – or plain guts?'

Thomson shrugged, and resumed work.

Presently, the runabout took shape between us. Simply, it was a large plastic bubble mounted on four outsize wheels, thick-tyred and independently sprung. Its five seats were each capacious enough to accommodate a space-suited man with all his gear. The battery and motor were mounted up front, and the bubble could be entered only through an airlock at the rear.

I was in the driving seat making final adjustments to the dashboard instruments when Marley's voice sounded impatiently from the radio.

'Marley calling ship. Marley calling ship.'

'Ship answering. Brunel here. Go ahead.'

'Why didn't you answer before, damn you?'

'Because the moon is round, damn you.'

'And made of green cheese,' added Thomson, over my shoulder.

The mike picked that up and Marley caught it.

'Oh, no, it isn't!' Triumph ousted impatience. 'It's made of gold. Rich, ripe, yellow gold. The Marleys have struck it richer than anyone did in the Yukon – or anywhere else. I'm telling you, Tycho's a gold-mine. All its streaks are pay-streaks. This is the bonanza to end all bonanzas.'

Maybe I should have become excited too, but I couldn't feel anything very much except some concern for Lou.

'Are you both all right?'

'Sure, but kind of tired; it's been a long walk. Lou, your man's worried about you. Tell him what it's like to feel on top of the world.'

'Were you *really* worried about me, Franz?'

It was good to hear her voice again.

'Frantically,' I said. 'We can't find where you left the tin-opener. However, just rest your feet now. The runabout's all fixed – I'll drive over and pick you up.'

'Okay, darling. Know where to find us? We're returning the way we went.'

'I'll find you.'

I crossed my fingers, then switched on the motor. It revved up with a buzz-saw noise that set your teeth on edge. Once warm, the motor quietened to a bearable hum. The designers had failed to eliminate that initial scream without at the same time trebling the misfire rate. It was a choice between irritants, and they chose the scream.

Thomson said, from the floor: 'Hold it a minute. There's just one more screw to this chair.'

'Aren't you coming along?'

'What – and leave Pettigue alone in the ship? Not on your life – and I mean your life. Next thing you know he'd blast off back to Earth and maroon us. Then he'd spin them some yarn back home about us being hit by meteorites: that would make a change from poisoned arrows. Or say we'd been wiped out by a volcanic eruption or something just as crazy. Believe me, Brunel, I'm serious about this. That nut has a psychotic compulsion to be the sole survivor. He just has to keep proving he's tougher or smarter than any bunch of heroes anywhere.'

The point was debatable but I wasn't inclined to start a debate at this time.

I pointedly waited for him to get out. He hesitated at the exit.

'You risking it without a suit? Clearplast is tough, I know, but it isn't proof against meteorites. You'll be riding in a bubble. If it's holed, you'll be a dead duck.'

He was right. It was taking a chance. But Lou had been taking chances out there for quite a while now. Her luck could run out while I prolonged her danger by delay over the tedious business of getting suited.

I said: 'Hurry it up, Tommy. Open the big door and let me out. Then make sure you keep in touch with us on the net.'

His smile had the now familiar twist of pain. 'You can't wait to see her again, can you? Oh, well, I know how it is.'

He got out, shutting the double doors of the runabout's little airlock, and quitted the garage – Pettigue had already done so. Soon afterwards, the wall facing me swung outward into the lunar night. The floor section began to move, taking the runabout with it through the aperture. For some moments I was suspended out there under the coal-black sky with its million hard, bright stars.

The section down-tilted, became a ramp. I eased off the brake. The tyres, ballooning higher than head-level, began to revolve and in no time were contacting the lunar surface. I slid the vehicle into gear.

As the first close-up photos showed long ago, the Mare Nubium was pitted with potholes averaging a yard in diameter and a couple of feet deep. The runabout's wheels and suspension were designed to make light of them and did; I never felt a jar.

Of course, the lesser gravity helped. When all four wheels left the ground because of some hump or depression taken at speed, the runabout's bound was long, shallow, gentle. After a series of these I felt as though I were traversing some enormous trampoline.

So this was the moon.

Even though (unlike a space-suit) the bubble in which I sat held off the vacuum at arm's length, providing a measure of detachment and illusory protection, I felt something of Pettigue's unease about being alone out here.

It was as though I were cut off from all human association. True, over my shoulder I could see Earth itself, the home of the race. But distance had shrunk it to a small impersonal object, no more real than a cardboard cut-out. Pale blue and vaguely configured, one side blotted out by night, it looked like half of a broken willow pattern plate perched on a high shelf: exotic and remote.

The unblinking stars were cold snakes' eyes watching the insect me scurrying across this vast and lifeless plain.

Just one mistake, they warned, just one accident cracking your frail bubble, just one unlucky hit, and you'll be as dead as the world you're on, a stone figure petrified in nothingness for all eternity.

My skin crawled.

There was a man in an outpost in the far north of Alaska who walked along in the long, long night under the silent slow-changing patterns of the Aurora Borealis. Awe came upon him. He became aware that the mysterious universe was inexorably overwhelming him, and diminishing him not merely as a person but also as a representative of his kind, by both its difference and indifference.

He described the feeling to me in a bar by Limehouse Reach.

I imaginatively sensed it then, and I actually sensed it now.

Maybe, scattered over immense stellar distances, mankind has potential friends. Maybe, again, he is all there is of his kind. How can he ever know? Outside the solar system stretched gulfs unthinkably wide and seemingly unbridgeable.

Sometimes it appeared to me that there were comparable gulfs between myself and my fellow men. I was unable to make contact. I had no real friends, and doubtless that was my own fault: I had more spines than a hedgehog and they were always at the on guard position.

I was a very lonely man until Lou came my way. Across the freezing gulf I had felt a breath of warmth at last. And now I was scared of losing this sole contact. So long as it existed my life, at any rate, held some meaning and the inscrutable universe's disregard of us all could itself be disregarded – much of the time, anyhow...

I peered ahead, searching for Lou in the Earthlight.

VIII

TWO PEOPLE TRIED TO SPEAK SIMULTANEOUSLY TO ISOLATED little me, blotting intelligibility from each other and sounding like a small angry mob.

'One at a time, please,' I said to the mike. 'Lou first.'

'Naturally,' Thomson whipped back, disobediently, sarcastically.

Lou said: 'You're way off beam, love. Alter course by ten or twelve degrees to your right.'

I obeyed, and sought her again. If she could see the runabout, then any time now I should be able to see her. Within seconds I picked up a tiny white speck near the horizon: it was probably both of them.

The guess was confirmed as I raced on. Slowly the speck enlarged and split in two.

'All right, Lou, I've got you in my sights.'

'And about time, Franz. It's been the other way round long enough.'

'I'll make up for it – don't worry. Off to you now. Tommy, what did you want?'

'Me? Nothing. Nothing I'm likely to find in this god-forsaken ash-heap. It's just that you told me to keep in touch – remember?'

Yes, I remembered. Poor devil, he was odd man out now, and keeping in touch with anyone at all was his problem.

'Okay, Tommy,' I said, quietly.

When I could discern the Marleys as shapes rather than specks, they appeared curiously squat. Then I realized that they were foreshortened, reclining and resting with feet towards me on the slope of a hump.

As the runabout covered the final couple of hundred yards, they arose and walked down the gentle slope to meet it. Each was carrying something which looked like a thick golden rod.

The slighter figure was Lou, of course: somehow she projected femininity even through her stiff-jointed space-suit. She made that anonymous, sexless thing walk like a woman. At least, so it seemed to me. Maybe my imagination contributed something.

Niggardly, I spared a brief glance for Marley. Obviously he was still full of excitement, but it was all inward now. He had his dreams, too, and his attention was absorbed by them. He was walking only automatically.

I drew up beside them. They entered separately through the small airlock at the rear. Lou flopped in the seat beside me, relaxing her grip on her golden rod. Slowly it became thicker, like an unrolling parchment.

I helped her to remove her helmet. Warm air wafted up from the collar. She was a bit flushed and perspiring. I held her tightly and kissed her. It was like trying to embrace an armoured Joan of Arc, but the kiss part of it was all right. She reacted as though we hadn't seen each other in months.

Then she murmured: 'It's wonderful, darling. I've never been so close to real happiness before.'

It was as though she'd assumed that happiness, by some natural law, was destined to be kept at arm's length from her, and that only now was it dawning on her that it could come within arm's reach.

Her father occupied best part of a brace of seats behind, still helmed, still silent in his wonderful private world.

Lou commented: 'He's just achieved his life's ambition. He'll never again be so happy as he is now.'

With a twinge of jealousy, I asked: 'You're so happy just because *he's* so happy?'

She smiled, and gently tweaked my nose. 'Only partly, dear. It's a double happiness. It's marvellous to be with you again. Dad's fulfilled himself. Now we're free to try for what we want in life.'

Mollified, I re-started the runabout. It screamed like a coursed hare. I headed it back to the ship.

Tommy called again: 'Found them yet, skipper?'

'Yes – they're both safely stowed aboard. We're just starting back.'

'Good. Congratulations to one and all.'

After a pause, he came again: 'Well, at least say hello, Lou.'

'Hello, Tommy,' she replied absently, caressing my jaw-line.

'Hello, goodbye, and out,' he said, curtly, sensing her indifference.

I began fingering the golden cylinder lying aslant my knee. It was composed of a score or so of thin sheets of what appeared to be beaten gold, rolled up together.

'These came from Tycho's rays?'

Lou nodded. 'The rays are a most peculiar formation. Made up of countless separate sheets, like those, lying flat but overlapping each other slightly... rather like fish-scales, except that they're diamond-shaped. They're not fused into the bedrock at all – at least, not in the area which we explored. You can detach them quite easily. They're as limp as gold leaf, and you can roll them up like newspapers.'

'Yes, they do resemble gold leaf. But *are* they gold?'

'Dad says they are, and he should know.'

'So should you,' I said, shrewdly.

'I haven't examined them all that closely.'

'Afraid of spoiling the dream?'

'I suppose so. But why shouldn't they be gold?'

I shrugged. 'So far as I know, it's never been found like this.'

'No, not on Earth, you idiot. But this is the moon. Even on Earth it's often been found as nuggets of pure gold. Under this much weaker gravitation it's conceivable that it could come in a less compact mould. Say, spewed out in streams from the Tycho crater, spreading itself thin. And then drying and hardening in scales like these.'

'Could be,' I admitted.

A voice spoke behind us, firm and loud. 'It is gold. There's no doubt of it.'

I glanced over my shoulder. Marley had removed his helmet and his eyes burned into mine.

'*Gold,*' he said.

Pettigue had been working in his cramped laboratory for more than half an hour.

Now he came to my cabin, slowly climbing up the connecting tube as though reluctant to reach the top of it.

Lou and I stared at him expectantly.

'It's *not* gold,' he mumbled.

Lou continued to stare at him, but her face was paler.

I said: 'I was afraid of that. What is it, then?'

'I can't say. Some new element, it seems. But certainly it's not gold – I've tried all the tests.'

I glanced at Lou. She still stared at Pettigue as though he were Thomson and she was half expecting him to give a silly guffaw and admit that he was only joking.

'Well, that's great,' I said. 'Marley's already told everyone back home that he's made the biggest gold strike ever.'

Pettigue said, miserably: 'I asked him to wait until I had verified it. But he just told me I was a fool, that if I couldn't recognize gold when I saw it then I didn't know my job. He said he didn't need to test it: he knew it was gold.'

'He always knew,' said Lou, tonelessly. 'He always knew it all.'

I sighed. 'Well, there's no dodging it. I'll have to go and tell him.'

'I'll tell him,' said Lou, dully.

'He'll about go off his head,' I warned. 'Better leave it to me.'

'It doesn't really concern you, Franz. It concerns him – and me. I grew up with this dream, you know. It won't be easy to uproot. He'll still going on believing in it though the heavens fall. And they may very well fall. It would be like him to pull them down on himself and on all of us, rather than face up to the truth.'

'Then it *does* concern me. And all of us, as you say. I'm coming with you. Pet, you'd better keep out of sight.'

Pettigue lifted his head and his opaque eyes looked right at me.

'I'm not skulking in any more corners any more, Captain. It's come to the point where I'd rather not live at all than go on dodging consequences. I have just passed a verdict and I want to be there to stand by it.'

I gripped his shoulder. 'There, I always said you had guts.'

Had I? Well, not exactly.

We came upon Marley down below at the radio extension in the big circular promenade. He was in the full spate of his triumph. Thomson lounged back, with crossed legs, on the couch watching him between boredom and cynicism.

'Yes, Sir Humphrey, it means that we're back on the Gold Standard and need never come off it. Just think what that means. Inevitably, trade will leap—'

Lou gently placed her palm over the mouth of the mike.

'Dad—'

Marley gripped her hand and crushed it so that she winced. He dragged it down to his side, and continued with hardly a pause: '—right up the chart. We can pay now – and make them pay. Excuse me, Sir Humphrey, something's just cropped up. I'll be back in a moment.'

He looked daggers at Lou.

'Just what are you trying to do to me?'

'Don't say any more, Dad, not just yet. It isn't gold. You mustn't make any more promises before we know where we stand.'

For a second his mouth hung slackly open. Then it closed in a tight line. His grim gaze passed from Lou to me, then to Pettigue.

'Pettigue,' he whispered, fiercely, 'Pettigue, I'll have your living heart for this, you utter fool.'

Then, calmly, into the mike: 'I'm sorry, Sir Humphrey, but I've been called away to deal with a matter that, unfortunately, seems to be of some urgency. So we'll have to resume this discussion later. Goodbye for now.'

He laid aside the mike and took a deep breath, gulping air like a skindiver just up from five fathoms. Then he exhaled with a sigh like Prometheus bracing himself against another liver attack.

He was a man given to exaggerating his reactions, and now he gave us yet another: the unnatural calm of a man forcing himself to be patient.

He breathed: 'Now perhaps someone will be good enough to explain?'

Lou told him: 'Pettigue's tests show that although the stuff looks like gold, actually it isn't.'

'Indeed? Then what do you say it is, Pettigue?'

Pettigue started to answer, looking at Marley's feet and stammering.

'What's that? Speak up, man!' Marley blasted away his own thin pretence of patience.

Pettigue's frail frame seemed to rock under the almost visible impact. And then his small limp hands clenched themselves. He raised his chin and stared Marley straight in the face.

'I don't say it's anything. Because I don't know what it is any more than you do. The reagents give no clue. In the Periodic Table—'

'You're trying to tell me it's a new element?'

'A new kind of metal, anyhow.'

'That's where you're mistaken, Pettigue. It's a very old kind of metal. It's gold. I've assayed gold a hundred times. I know the look, the feel, the very smell of it. I'm telling you it's gold.'

'You can tell me, Colonel Marley. And you can believe it if you wish. But that doesn't make it true.'

Pettigue was standing up to him at last. It's a long worm that has no turning, and Pettigue was beginning to turn. Silently, I was rooting for him.

Marley was aware of it, too: opposition from the least expected quarter. His eyes half closed as he reassessed both Pettigue and the position.

Then he said, about mellifluously as a rusty hinge: 'All right, let's just suppose it isn't gold. Then I've made a fool of myself in front of the whole world, haven't I? The biggest laughing stock of all time. You're the official metallurgist of this party, and you stood aside and let me do just that.'

'That's a bloody lie!' cried Lou. 'He asked you to wait until he'd completed testing. But no, you couldn't wait. You *knew*, didn't you? Well, you didn't. For once, you damn well didn't.'

Marley didn't even turn his head.

'You wanted me to walk right into it, Pettigue. So you let me. Hoist with my own petard, eh? But I still think it's you who's made the mistake, little fellow. And, by God, if you have, the world will soon know all about it. Your professional reputation, such as it is, won't be worth last year's calendar. You'd better go back to your reagents and do your homework again. But I tell you this: whatever answer you come up with, you're finished. If it is gold, after all, you've cut your own throat. And if it isn't, I shan't cover up for you. I'll tell them how you misled me, how you let me assume that it was.'

I just gasped, but Thomson sat up straight on the couch and said: 'Heaven knows I'm no George Washington, but even I could never hope to dream up such a blatant perversion of the facts.'

I found my voice, and said: 'You can't expect to get away with that one, Marley.'

But he didn't look at us. Nor even at Pettigue any more. Only at Lou. He was waiting the only verdict he seemed to care about.

Her eyes were full of sorrow.

She said, haltingly: 'Dad, I was so glad for you… and proud of you… back there. I thought, despite the rest of it, you were truly great. A big man. And now… you've spoilt it all. You're your own worst enemy. People don't need to try to cut you down to size. You do it to yourself.'

Marley sighed once more. A monstrous sound, like Atlas shouldering the burden again. He became withdrawn and oblivious to us all, even Lou.

When he spoke it was softly to himself, as though he were musing in a desert or solitary on the ramparts of Elsinore.

'In the end, there's nobody – nobody but yourself. You're as big or small as you think you are. You're as right or wrong as you believe yourself to be. Believe, and you shall be saved. Believe, and the world believes with you – and accepts you at your own valuation. Against its prejudices, against its will, maybe, and even against the so-called facts. For facts in the final analysis are only beliefs. Belief is everything. The great man can make anyone believe anything. I believe I am a great man, because that I *have* to believe. The categorical imperative. Therefore, they will believe me, because I believe. They will believe *me...*'

He wandered slowly away and went from our sight around the sweep of the tubular ring.

'Pure paranoia,' commented Thomson, shaking his head.

Pettigue, grim and silent, walked off stiffly in the opposite direction, towards his cabin.

Lou looked so forlorn that I clasped her comfortingly.

She whispered: 'He's gone away from me again, Franz. I'd thought, out there, it would never happen any more. For the first time since he used to play make-believe games with me in the nursery we were *sharing* something completely. The great adventure, the search for the Holy Grail. And then came the miracle: we found it together. *His* Holy Grail, anyhow. It was marvellous. No more disappointments, no more frustration. You should have seen the way it transformed him. I've never seen him so relaxed, never known him so mellow and warm. There was a place for affection, maybe even love, again. But the Grail turned out to be only fairy gold, after all. Everything's worse than it was before.'

I said, soothingly: 'He'll get over it. The born prospector never gives up. The flash in the pan passes and is forgotten.'

'Wrong metaphor, old man,' said Thomson, disconcertingly. 'Wrong flash, wrong pan.'

I frowned at him over Lou's shoulder, and resumed: 'Sooner or later, he'll hit a new trail – you'll see.'

'He's right there, though,' said Thomson. 'To travel hopefully, etcetera. The excitement of the chase is what really matters to those types. The kill is always an anti-climax. Frankly, Lou, this gold bug thing seems to me a mere side issue. This isn't a gold rush, you know. We're supposed to be astronauts, not argonauts. This is supposed to be part of the much greater adventure of the exploration of space. What about your own particular Holy Grail? Have you looked for any trace of organic life on this celestial dust-bowl? No, you've subordinated everything to the puerile obsessions of your old man. But he never gave you or your work a thought. Didn't that show you how petty he is? It's time you quit the nursery and those make-believe games, Lou.'

'Shut up, Tommy,' I said – belatedly, because in the main I went along with him.

Lou tore herself free from me, and for a moment I thought she was going to hit him. But she checked herself. She stood over him, shaking with cold anger. 'All right, he's a little man with big ideas. But you're even less than that: a little man with little ideas. At least he went out on a limb after his big idea. You've never even started to climb any tree.'

'I leave that to the monkeys, old girl. Look where it's landed him, anyway. The limb busted and dropped him right in the soup.'

'Yes, and doesn't that make you feel good? You're laughing all the way up your yellow streak, aren't you?'

Thomson went a bit pale. He stood up.

'Some day I'll cut those claws of yours, Lou.'

'Watch out for yourself when you try it: they're tipped with curare. I haven't forgotten what you did to poor harmless little Mack. So be careful – I'm a cat of a different colour.'

'All right, both of you – that's enough,' I said. 'We're all edgy because we're all tired. Nobody's had any real sleep for a couple of days. Now hear this: get to your bunks and relax for a few hours. You'll feel better afterwards. I'm going to turn in myself.'

Thomson hesitated, then said: 'Probably a correct diagnosis, skipper. I know I shan't need any sleeping pills. See you later.'

With a parting hard look at Lou, he went.

Lou combed her hair back with her fingers and darted a glance at me. I smiled.

'Oh, dear,' she said, 'I'll never be the captain's lady. I'll always be tangling with people and letting you down, Franz.'

'Never mind, I'll probably be right in there with you. I'm not a good mixer, either.'

She tugged at my arm.

'Come on, dear – let's go to bed.'

'Sure, I'm going to bed – *my* bed. To sleep, perchance to dream. But certainly to sleep. My God, I'm tired.'

She said: 'So am I, but I'm worried about the spot Dad's got himself in. I shan't be able to sleep a wink alone. I'll just lie there. I need solacing. I need love and to feel there's someone at my side.'

'I said no. Not this time.'

She spat at me: 'What a mouldy old ruin of a tower of strength you've turned out to be!'

'Like Tommy?'

'Like all men. You're a selfish, untrustworthy species. I was a fool to think of marrying any one of you. I should have learned from my mother's experience what to expect.'

She flounced off to her cabin.

I made one of those Well-that's-women-for-you expressive shrugs to my nil audience. Then flipped on the radio to inform the Earthlings that we would be remaining off the ether for a few hours. I flipped it off again even more quickly, before any questions cropped up or I got buttonholed by one of Marley's titled friends.

Then I made a round of the ship. Everyone had retired to their cabins.

The last cabin I investigated was Lou's. My behaviour had been rather harsh, I decided. I intended to offer an apology or even the doubtful benefit of my company, after all. I was prepared for any kind of reception, but not for the sight of Lou curled up on her bunk fast asleep.

I kissed her lightly. She didn't stir. I guessed she must be physically and emotionally exhausted, so I left her to sleep in peace.

Outside my own cabin door I paused to consider. If I went to bed now, everyone would be off duty at the same time. I ought to arrange a guard roster. At least one person should remain awake and alert.

Alert for what, though? There were no Indians on the moon. Nor anything that breathed or moved.

Those who were still awake were in no mood to discuss rosters. Those who slept were out to the world. I was dog-tired myself and knew I couldn't keep my eyes open for much longer.

So I skipped it and went to my own bunk.

Another of my sins of omission, another black mark on the record of Captain Brunel.

Hours later, Lou shook me awake.

'Franz, have you seen Dad?'

I struggled up on to one elbow. My arm tingled with pins and needles.

'What?'

'Have you seen Dad? I can't find him anywhere.'

I rubbed my eyes to see her more clearly. She looked just as worried as she sounded.

'No, I've been asleep. Isn't he in his cabin? I saw him there before I came to bed.'

I got to my feet.

'Let's check the space-suits.'

'Surely he wouldn't—'

But I was already out of the door. She caught up with me in the space-suit bay.

I pointed to the gap. 'One missing – his.'

She bit her lip. 'I shouldn't have left him alone in that state of mind. I'm worried. He could have gone a little crazy and—'

'Have you seen Pettigue and Tommy?'

'Yes, they were asleep, too. They've not seen or heard anything of him. They're going to look for him. But I'm sure he's not anywhere in the ship: I've been all over.'

'Is the runabout still in the garage?'

'Yes.'

'H'm. Then it looks as if he's gone for a walk out there.'

'He's gone back to that damned goldfield,' she said, suddenly. 'I should have guessed. Trying again. Hoping that he just struck unlucky last time. Hoping to find the real stuff this time. You were right, Franz – they never give up.'

'If he was that keen to go back, why didn't he take the runabout?

It's so much quicker. Why walk all that way, especially as it half-killed him the last time?'

'I suspect that's the whole point of it, Franz. He would think that doing it the easy way would be a kind of cheating. He would imagine his grandfather laughing him to scorn – the pan-handler in the automobile. In the Yukon they broke the trail on foot, through six kinds of hell. Dad always wanted to do what his grandpa had done – only strike it bigger and richer and keep his hands on it.'

I suppose I looked unconvinced.

She said: 'All right, it sounds pretty silly. But he's a romantic. Dreams are real to him. A part of him is always living in the Yukon of his imagination.'

'Yes, I know. That blow to his dream must have really hit him. Confused him, too. He could be confusing dream with reality somewhere out there now.'

That's what I said, and maybe there was truth in it. All the same, Marley seemed to me a man who knew exactly what he was doing in the contemporary world also. He wanted to slip away on his private journey without any of us knowing he'd gone. And he was aware that if he took the runabout, the shriek of its starting would awaken every one of us.

But I left that unsaid, and instead suggested: 'We best go after him. I'll try not to tread on his dreams, but I just don't want any of my crew wandering about on their own without my knowing what they're up to.'

'You're right, Franz.'

It was nice to know that this time she was on my side.

At the garage entrance we bumped into Thomson and Pettigue. Thomson reported: 'He's nowhere around, Captain.'

'No, he's left the ship. Lou and I are going out after him. Get on the net and keep in contact. Then if he does happen to come back while we're searching in the wrong direction, you can let us know.'

'Sure, I'll do that.' He went off.

Pettigue just stood there like a wooden Indian. I couldn't think of anything useful that a wooden Indian could do at this time, so left him standing there.

Lou and I, space-suited in the runabout, headed for the nearest point of Tycho's ray. We found Marley along the trail, only a mile from the ship.

He was lying on his back, staring up at a billion stars and unable to see any one of them.

We stood over him. His countenance was visible through the face-plate like that of a corpse in a coffin in the Latin countries. Indeed, he was in his coffin. The death-glaze was on the eyes open in a swollen, blood-red face.

The cooling system of his suit had failed and he had broiled himself with his own body heat. His mouth was open in the ultimate gasp.

Marley was dead. Like Scrooge's partner, Marley was as dead as a door-nail.

A terrible sound came to my ears. A dry sobbing, like the painful racking of the death-rattle from a throat denied moisture.

Lou was broadcasting her grief. I wanted to grant her privacy, indicate to her to switch off her microphone. But I couldn't bring myself to intrude on her even that much. Anyhow, I was sure she was oblivious to me and to everything except her dead father.

Disturbedly, I endured her pain. We were sealed apart by more than merely our space-suits.

Thomson's voice came through: 'What's happening out there? Anything gone wrong?'

I said: 'We've found Colonel Marley. I'm afraid he's dead. Leave it be now, Tommy. We'll bring him back.'

Silence. Then: 'All right, Franz.' And silence again.

No hint of regret. No condolences for Lou. No emotion at all, not even surprise. I recalled his prediction of death coming among us. Probably this lack of reaction was just fatalistic acceptance.

I knelt awkwardly to examine the few outer controls on Marley's suit. This standard suit had been designed by the Farnborough boffins. It depended on water-cooling, which had proved superior to air-cooling with its risk of dehydration. The water was circulated through tubes threaded through a garment worn next to the skin. A small pump powered this flow and was regulated by a knob.

To keep the skin temperature down to a bearable 80 degrees F. during periods of physical exertion, one had to keep adjusting this knob. If it jammed, the consequences could be serious.

The knob on Marley's suit had jammed. The cause became immediately obvious. Wrapped tightly around it, clogging the screw thread, was a single sheet of the fairy gold, crumpled and rolled into a long twist of soft metal, resembling wire.

I tried to unwind it and pull it free. The thick material of my space-suit gloves made this delicate operation extremely difficult. I couldn't get a grip on the clinging strand. Marley must have tried similarly, though much more desperately. And similarly failed.

I abandoned it and stood up. I had no theory about it. Theories could wait.

*

I don't wish to dwell on that nightmare-like journey back to the ship. Marley, still in his suit, lay in the back of the runabout, and Lou stayed as motionless and silent beside him.

It was as though I were driving a hearse across that dead plain.

Conflicting feelings were pulsing through my nerves. The sheer pressure of the overload made me try to exclude them *en bloc*.

I was sorry about Marley. I had never really liked him, and most of the time I had hated him. But now I was sorry that this had happened to him. That kind of slow death shouldn't happen to anyone.

So there was regret.

Also, there was curiosity. What had happened? Almost certainly he had set out, playing the rôle of the lone prospector, intent on revisiting what he still hoped would prove to be a goldfield.

Then, warming up through the exertion of hard walking, he'd tried to cool off. And found the control jammed. The excess heat couldn't escape and was beginning to stifle him. After failing to free the knob, he turned back in panic, aiming to regain the safety of the ship. More exertion, more excess heat unable to flow away – until the rise in body temperature became fatal.

Curiosity was quelled by remorse.

Through his radio, Marley must have called the ship again and again, frantically calling for help.

But we were deaf, because we were asleep.

It was my fault that everyone was sleeping and no-one was on watch. Indirectly, I had killed Lou's father.

Curiosity forced its way back to attention. Indirectly, I had killed Marley. But who had *directly* killed him by jamming that control?

Again I tried to close my mind against these disturbing thoughts. But another kept slipping past the barrier.

What was going on in Lou's mind? I couldn't even guess. But I felt that I knew what was in her heart.

Remorse. Far, far more intense than my own.

Whether she had even noted, much less grasped the significance of, the cause of her father's death I didn't know. As we had carried Marley between us into the vehicle, she uttered no sound except this awful crying.

She had said no word to me since the discovery, and when the crying died away she remained dumb.

But I had detected a quality in that crying which intimated the presence of more than grief at bereavement. There was this keen and self-torturing remorse. Remorse either for what she had done or (like my own) for what she had omitted to do.

IX

WE BURIED MARLEY ON THE MOON.

Lou was next of kin and wanted it that way. He was not the first man to be interred on our satellite – two Americans and a Russian had preceded him – but it was still some kind of distinction. The posthumous kind was all he could expect now. I guessed Lou regarded it as a small compensation for the fame he missed.

I had to guess, because Lou had ceased to confide anything to me. She'd retired into introspection. I made no attempt to shake her out of it: I knew I couldn't reach her. Eventually she must emerge, but as what kind of personality I could only conjecture.

I hoped she would be my own girl again, because I missed her badly. She was light-years away from me now, and I was alone again. This brooding, withdrawn Lou was like a stranger.

To save labour – for labour when one is space-suited is hard graft indeed – we used one of the countless tiny craterlets for a grave. Of course, we shaped it to the conventional rectangle, with pick and drill, and shovelled out the pervading loose dust.

Temporarily I turned preacher and intoned the burial service. Well, approximately. I had done my best to memorize it, for it was all but impossible to read from the book under the prevailing conditions.

After which, I became a labourer again and helped the others raise a cairn of rock fragments over the grave.

For a short while, then, we stood beside the cairn silent with our thoughts. The monolithic ship dwarfed our little monument and us, too. The *mare* stretched drably around us on all sides, grey as our mood. The Pacific Ocean shone like a polished silver crescent in the dark sky. On the duller, cloud-blurred land masses up there men were moving in their millions about their business...

But Marley's business was ended.

Unfortunately, my business with Marley was not.

I had reported to my Space Service chiefs that Marley had died because of a failure of operation in the cooling system in his suit. That was true, but not the whole truth.

It was my business to try to uncover the whole truth.

I had already begun it by uncovering Marley. I had commandeered Thomson's aid to get Marley's body free from the suit. He, after all, was the doctor. He examined it and certified the cause of death to be heat stroke, which was close enough.

After the funeral, I retired to my cabin and started in on the brainwork. I reviewed the possibilities one at a time, and eventually the list grew even longer than my face.

First: accidental death. The gold sheet (to call it that) had become accidentally wrapped around the control knob.

This was a short journey down a short *cul-de-sac*. My imagination could conceive no convincing picture of the thing happening accidentally. The stuff was wound around the thread too tightly and too thoroughly for it to have got there by chance.

All right, then, a variation: accidental death arising from a stupid joke. This theory pointed straight to Thomson, the incurable *farceur*. Relations between Marley and him had soured on this trip and he had fallen out of favour.

Presumably this rankled. He had to get a bit of his own back, in his characteristic way. So he fixed Marley's suit, expecting to make the owner stew uncomfortably for a while – ironically, through the agency of a piece of his own fairy gold. But not expecting Marley to venture out alone, nor foreseeing the stuff would be impossible to remove when wearing gloves.

Well, it was feasible. Thomson could be that kind of short-sighted fool, especially after a few drinks.

What other possibility? Suicide? For what reason?

Marley had thought that at last he had reached El Dorado. In the very moment of triumph, the dream was blown to pieces. And the whole world was about to learn that it was through his own silly blundering. Dazed by the disaster, yet proud as Lucifer, he couldn't face the coming humiliation. So he took this way out, making it look like an accident.

Two things were wrong with that theory.

First, it *didn't* look like an accident. There were simpler and more convincing ways of staging an 'accidental' death. Quicker, less painful ones, too. For instance, he could have punctured his space-suit to simulate meteoric penetration and died almost instantaneously.

Second, as I had said before, the born prospector never gives up. In this direction Marley was a monomaniac. His confidence might have taken a beating, but would never shatter completely. I believed he took that trail again assured that somehow he would yet find gold at the end of it.

Well, that left the remaining possibility, the dirty word: murder. Which postulated a murderer.

Mentally, I put Thomson on trial again.

If he had no love for Marley, he also had no motive for murdering him that I could see. For in what way could that possibly benefit him? It would certainly not help him to win Lou back.

Well, then, Pettigue. But he'd said he could never bring himself to kill another man. Again, he'd also said that maybe you could only become a man by doing just that. Certainly he longed to become a man, a real man, instead of an apology for one.

Another motive: Marley had always bullied him cruelly, and had just threatened to ruin his professional reputation and so take away his last – and probably only – shred of self-respect.

On top of that, Thomson held that Pettigue *was* a killer, in a devious kind of way.

On the other hand, it was hard to imagine anyone who looked and behaved less like a murderer than Pettigue… until you remembered Dr Crippen.

Yes, I must regard Pettigue as a suspect.

Then there was Lou. My thoughts became confused by emotion however detachedly I tried to consider her. And they flung up a protective barrier against the awful idea of parricide.

During this turmoil Thomson climbed the tube to my cabin and paused on the rungs, peering over the rim at me.

'Can I see you, Captain, or are you busy?'

'You can see me and I *am* busy.'

He came in.

'It seems to me that this is a pretty sticky situation,' he said.

'I was just thinking the same thing.'

'I didn't like to broach it before the funeral was over, but we'll have to get to the bottom of the cause of Marley's death.'

I pointed to Marley's space-suit, which I'd carried up here – it would be Exhibit A at the unavoidable inquest.

'Take a look at that pump control knob, and you'll see the cause.'

'I didn't mean that, Franz. We all know about that. I'll put it another way. Who, in your opinion, was responsible for Marley's death?'

'Initially Marley himself, for ignoring my orders.'

'That's beside the point. He didn't wittingly kill himself. Somebody laid for him.'

'I assume you exonerate yourself, Doctor?'

'"Doctor", is it? We're very formal. I gather you're set on a formal investigation, as they phrase it. All right, fair enough. Naturally I exonerate myself. I'm no murderer.'

'No. I don't think you are. Not intentionally, anyhow. Now, let's be serious about this, Tommy. Answer me plainly before we go any further. Was this an unfortunate sequel to one of your practical jokes?'

'No. Is that plain enough? I'll say it again. No.'

'Very well. Then do you know anything at all, any little thing, that might give me a lead? For instance, did you hear anyone moving around during the rest period?'

'No, not even Marley himself. I slept like the dead... with all due respects to the dead. I know nothing – which is less, maybe, than you do.'

I looked at him appraisingly. That humorous set of his eyes imputed humour to a remark I didn't think funny.

'What do you mean by that, Tommy?'

He shrugged.

'It was you and Lou who found Marley, you know. Already dead, you say.'

'You doubt that?' I asked angrily. 'You suspect I killed him and Lou's covering up for me?'

'Don't get worked up, old man. How could I possibly accuse Lou of covering up when she hasn't said a damn word to anyone? Or hardly. She's still in a state of shock. Or trauma, if you like. And of course I don't suspect you of murder. You know very well who I *do* suspect.'

'Pettigue, no doubt.'

He nodded. 'I told you, and you wouldn't believe me. Now I tell you for the last time. He has this mad compulsion. All our lives are in danger while he goes unwatched and unguarded. This is what I've come to beg you to do: keep him locked in his cabin until we get back to Earth. Otherwise, we shall never get back.'

I considered, and found myself gnawing a knuckle.

I said: 'I've no grounds for putting him under close arrest, any more than I have for doing the same to you. You've built up a case against Pet from pure assumption, based on nothing more than the fact that you don't like or understand him. In short, you fear what you don't know.'

'Do you like or understand him, Franz?'

'Not to any great extent, admittedly. But more than you do.'

'And you refuse to restrain him?'

'There's no choice.'

'Well, I'm not warning you again. After this, I think only of little me and saving my own skin. I've a hunch that I'm the next on the list.'

He turned to leave.

'Hold it a minute,' I said. 'You told me a while back that Lou once nearly killed her father. Now, I'm not asking out of mere curiosity nor do I really believe it has any relevance. It's just that I have to cover all the angles. So, what were the circumstances?'

He surveyed me with the old mockery.

'Don't tell me that you're harbouring suspicions about your lady love—'

'Shut up!' I said, savagely.

'Okay.'

Again he turned to go.

'No, wait.' I began pacing the confined circle of the cabin. 'Look, Tommy,' I flung at him, 'leave your feelings out of it just this once. Simply remember that you're the ship's medico and I need your professional assistance. Lou is – and we both know it – a disturbed personality. Her parents tore her to pieces between them. That kind of thing leads to schizophrenia, doesn't it?'

'It certainly does, old man.'

'Then do you think it possible that at times of intense emotional upset she's capable of doing things she's not consciously aware of? I mean, things she wouldn't normally dream of doing—'

'Like killing her father, Franz? Hell, she's dreamt of it often enough – I can tell you that, without going into details. As for the time she actually tried it… well, my father was the family doctor then. Lou was sixteen. That's always an unstable age for adolescents, particularly females. It was then she discovered how her father had framed and destroyed her mother. She went clean off her head. Flew at him with a knife. Gashed his throat. My father saved his life, but it was a near thing.'

I came to a halt.

'And you married her, knowing that?'

'I couldn't help it, old man. I was infatuated with her. Old Marley encouraged me, too. Keep the secret in the family sort of thing. Apart from that, he rather liked the idea of having a strain of the blood of the ancient lairds infused into the Marley clan. Lou was right about that. She was wrong about my marrying for money, though: I never gave it a thought. I just wanted her.'

'I see. Well, thanks, Tommy.'

'That's all right. But if you're chasing the idea that Lou's some kind of Jekyll and Hyde case, you're on the wrong track, in my opinion.'

'The right track being Pettigue?'

'No question about it. Again, in my opinion.'

He lowered himself into the tubular exit.

Alone, I assumed various postures associated with deep thought, but deep thought remained elusive. So I phoned around the ship for Pettigue and located him in his lab. I asked him to come and see me.

He arrived wearing his old hang-dog aspect. Bad habits are the devil to slough off, and I wondered if he were still making the effort. I felt like snapping: 'For Pete's sake, Pet, look at me. I'm right here – not two paces to my left nor lying on the floor.'

But that sounded too much like an echo of Marley.

So I just asked, quietly. 'What are you working at, Pettigue?'

He addressed my console. 'Oh, mineral specimens. Those I collected and, of course, the new element.'

'It *is* a new element?'

'Unquestionably. There's nothing resembling its structure on Earth, so far as we know.'

'Then surely it's at least as valuable as gold,' I said. 'And Colonel Marley did, in fact, stumble on a kind of gold-mine.'

'Not necessarily. It's not unusual in the field of atomics for new elements to be created artificially. Rarity in itself doesn't mean much. A material's monetary value is geared to the uses it can be put to. Gold is quite another matter. Like diamonds, it's accepted as a general medium of exchange.'

'I see. What about your other specimens? Anything interesting to report?'

'Not really, Captain. They're much the same sort of stuff that the Americans and Russians found in their areas. Miss Marley confirms my findings. She's working with me.'

'She is?' This was news. And good news, surely. If she were beginning to take an interest in the external world again... well, I was part of that world, too.

I indulged myself in some wishful thinking.

Presently, Pettigue asked: 'Will that be all, Captain?'

'Er – there's one other thing. I was wondering if by any chance you have any comment to make concerning Colonel Marley's death.'

At last he met my gaze.

'What kind of comment, Captain? A confession, maybe?'

I laughed uneasily, feeling sure now that he *had* overheard Thomson broadcast his opinion that Pettigue was a homicidal maniac, and feeling equally unsure of how to answer him. So I didn't.

'The only confession I can make,' he said after my false laughter died, 'is that I feel unable to mourn that man's death. But concerning the reasons for his death, I know absolutely nothing.'

'Well, then, that's that,' I said, wanting to end it now. 'Thanks for being frank, anyhow. You can return to your work now.'

He nodded curtly and departed.

So nobody knows anything, I told myself, except maybe Lou. And I don't believe she knows anything, either.

For from her demeanour on our joint search for Marley I judged she no more anticipated its shocking climax than I had.

One nagging thought still remained, though: the fact that multiple personalities were not always conscious of the existence of each other on varying levels. When one personality was in control of the body, the submerged others were often not cognizant of its actions. I began to recall some of the documented cases I'd read about...

However painful it might prove, for either or both of us, it was my duty to question Lou.

In the event, it was Lou who began to question me.

More precisely, it was L. A. Marley who interrogated me. L. A. Marley, the distinguished biochemist, who had returned from a past I'd never known. However, I soon placed her by the description Tod Reeves, the science editor, had given me on the day I first met Lou. 'A fine male mind functioning in a fine female body. Striking, remarkable – but quite unattainable.'

I was sitting at the radio when she came into my life, and doing a sub-standard job of making bricks without straw. In short, making my required daily report with nothing to report.

The awareness of this grave person standing over me, silently but attentively listening, eroded my none too impregnable confidence. She stood so erect that she seemed taller than Lou. Her hair was drawn back tightly in a masculine – almost – style that I didn't like. Even less did I like the general air of authority she wore, the coolly watchful eyes, the impression that my performance was being judged.

She reminded me of a female teacher who had a way, without ever actually voicing anything condemnatory, of making me feel an even smaller infant than I was at the time.

Miss Perkins.

Sometimes I suspected that my dislike of women and of authority all began with Miss Perkins.

I stumbled on self-consciously with my report, which came to no conclusion: it merely stopped when I ran out of alibis.

'Is that all?' asked a faintly incredulous, faintly disapproving voice from Technical Information H.Q.

Caught between two fires, I snarled: 'Yes, that's all.'

L. A. Marley said, without urgency, in the Girton accent which made my snarl sound by contrast pure animal: 'Not quite all, Captain Brunel. My report on mineral analysis is ready for transmission and may be of some interest.'

(Implying the unsaid postscript: 'As opposed to your puerile drivel.')

'Interest to who?' I meant to sound dispassionate, but the snarl was still there.

'To whom?' (I winced.) 'Why, to your goodself, I trust.'

I snatched the written leaves from her.

She regarded her suddenly empty hand expressionlessly, then patiently put it behind her, together with her other unemployed one, and waited for my comments on her work.

These were not forthcoming, as I discovered that quite two-thirds of the report was in mathematical symbols.

I let a fair-sized stretch of eternity tick away as I stared at them, then said: 'You really think you have something here?'

'What do *you* think, Captain?'

'I think you'd better transmit this report yourself,' I said, rising, 'because I don't understand a bloody equation of it.'

In a single movement she took both the report and my seat.

'Perhaps I better had,' she said, with a frigid condescension that made me want to grab her and crush her until either I'd frightened her back into becoming a child or roused her into becoming a woman. I knew the child. And I knew the woman. I understood them. L. A. Marley I neither knew nor understood.

She flicked the radio alive again with the finger of a practised technician.

'*Endeavour* calling Technical Information H.Q. This is L. A. Marley...'

It certainly was. I took my discomfiture out into the great ring and completed a dozen laps with it at an angry stride.

I re-entered the radio room in time to catch the end of her report which, unlike mine, existed and was crisp and succinct: 'It has been decided to call this new element Marlionum. M-A-R-L-I-O-N-U-M. Will you repeat that?'

The voice from T.I., H.Q. did so, respectfully.

'Correct. End of report. Out.'

L. A. Marley squared the loose sheets and stood up. I wished she hadn't. It put me below her head level.

'Whom – who decided to call it Marlionum?' I asked, sternly.

'I did, Captain. I named it after my father, who discovered it. Mr Pettigue also thought it suitable.'

'Why was I not consulted?'

She raised one eyebrow all of an eighth of an inch.

'Because it was no concern of yours.'

'I should point out that, as commander of this expedition now that Colonel Marley is dead, every matter relating to it concerns me.'

'Yes, Captain, you *should* point that out – to yourself, to begin with. Let me be frank. This is supposed to be a scientific expedition. In my opinion, it should be headed by a qualified scientist. Or, at least, someone who comprehends what the scientific method means. As it is, no systematic work has been done and everything's been allowed to slide into chaos. I'm doing my best to get things organized, with some slight assistance from Mr Pettigue. But the true responsibility is yours – and what are *you* doing?'

What I was doing, actually, was gasping for breath. She'd taken mine away.

She continued, smoothly, answering her own question: 'Nothing, so far as I can see, except to try to maintain a pretence that everything's under control. I don't say it's entirely your fault. The job was thrust upon you, and it's too bad that you're not the right person for it. All the same, you could make some sort of effort to interest yourself in it. For instance, here's me – an underling – preparing and sending reports on the Marlionum Deposit, while you, the boss, haven't even bothered to go out there and inspect it. Have you, Captain?'

I shook my head, dumbly.

'Then you should go. And consider yourself honoured. It's a unique discovery. My father's name will live long after yours has faded into oblivion. Another thing: Dr Thomson appears to be merely a passenger on this trip. We can't afford to carry passengers. Can't you find some useful work for him? If you can't, I can.'

'You can?'

I wasn't really asking. The utterance was mechanical, a stopgap to give me time to get on to the L. A. Marley wavelength.

'I can and shall,' she said, firmly.

She made as if to pass me.

I put out a hand. 'Before you go, tell me something. Have you any idea how your father's death came about? I'm sorry if this seems—'

'It was death by misadventure,' she interrupted. 'Or so the court will term it. A better term would be "death by adventure". For he was an adventurer who died on his greatest adventure. Now, if you'll excuse me—'

I stood aside. She brushed past and I felt no response to the touch of her. She was asexual as the white lab. coat she wore. The long fingers which had sent electric shocks through me now seemed intended only to measure their strength with a voltmeter. She could have been made of plastic. Certainly, she had no more feeling or sympathetic understanding than a doll.

A doll with a brain – and nothing else.

Nothing else, I divined, because she couldn't bear the agony of being anything more. Lou had been drugged at her own request and shut away in a private ward. This isolated and frozen fragment of pre-frontal brain matter was her guardian, who registered my I.Q. with a comptometer and deduced that that tiny total was all there was of me.

Surely, the L. A. Marley who wrote the books and corresponded with the scientific big bugs must have been a little more human than this limited creature? Else she could not have kept her correspondents, and certainly not any friendly correspondents, for long.

I recalled that she didn't keep her husband for long.

I decided to consult that one-time husband again.

'L. A. Marley? My God, yes,' said Tommy, at ease on his bunk, his hands clasped behind his head and one foot swinging freely. 'That bitch was responsible for our divorce in the end. She never thought much of me in those days, and obviously she still doesn't.'

'You've met the re-incarnation?'

'Briefly. For about five minutes. She cross-examined me, about my activities or the lack of them. I'm afraid I didn't respond very intelligently – that is, by her standards. She has no humour, you know; a flippant answer is marked in her book as a wrong answer. Either you're right or you're wrong: there are no half-truths. I must admit I was a bit shaken to see L. A. Marley making a comeback. At least, to begin with. But, even after only a few minutes, I could tell she wasn't really the genuine article. Only a sketchy caricature of the original – I couldn't take her seriously. The one I'd tried to live with was a real person: three-dimensional. She could strike me with terror, admiration, or despair – sometimes all three at the same time. She was a hard worker, but I liked it best when she wasn't working.'

'Why then?'

'Because then, old man, she didn't exist. L. A. Marley was like – hell, like a water fountain: she existed only while she was working. When she wasn't, I had a wife who was a woman, and we could laugh together and have fun and games. But I could seldom hold that woman for long. Guess I was short on magnetic attraction... or something. Anyway, she kept going back to work. Sometimes she shut herself away for weeks in her study or lab., working like a dedicated robot.'

'That must have been hard to take.'

'It was, Franz. In the end she drove me to look for companion-ship elsewhere. Female companionship, I mean, of course. That was the *prima facie* reason for divorce.'

I said: 'Well, we sure live and learn. I had no idea things were like that. I'm beginning to believe there are two sides to every divorce.'

'You have to make allowances for Lou. She can't help her selves. I tried to help them, but they were too much of a handful for me. I was never much good at stopping dog-fights.'

'Someone's got to stop this one, Tommy.'

'You think you're the man to do it?'

'I don't know about that. I only know I'm the man who's going to have to try. For two good reasons: I love Lou and I'm damned if I'm going to let L. A. Marley blot her out of existence. The other reason is that I doubt if Lou can ever be cured – become integrated, that is – until the cause of Marley's death is brought out into the open. Whether she had anything to do with it or not, God knows. But I believe that in some strange way she's blaming herself for it. And so she's condemned herself to extinction behind this façade of L. A. Marley.'

'Façade,' nodded Thomson. 'That's the word I should have used instead of caricature. You know, L. A. Marley began to manifest herself soon after the traumatic shock Lou went into following her attempt to kill her old man. The cool young student of science, dwelling in a world where things could be weighed, measured, labelled, and pigeon-holed. So that you could count on them not to let you down by changing into something horribly different. Where the laws are immutable and couldn't be twisted and used to hurt someone you love. The sane, ordered world of mathematics where there couldn't be any injustice. So permitting L. A. Marley to go on living with her father, whom Lou hated and had tried to kill, and because of that felt remorse and guilt, because she also loved him. Am I confusing you?'

'No, on the contrary,' I said, slowly. 'It's damnably involved, but it makes sense. It's a mirror of the current situation. In a bizarre way, history is repeating itself. Lou finds her father violently killed. The shock is associated in her mind with the old trauma of her adolescence. It sets up the same kind of pattern. Remorse, withdrawal, and concealment behind another person. So what happens now?'

Thomson shrugged.

'I suppose it depends on what happened before,' I said.

Thomson shook his head.

'No, you can't use the past to predict the future, Franz. Too many factors are different. Marley's really dead this time, for one thing. Another new factor is Lou's feelings towards you. I suspect that she doesn't want to lose you, either, and that's why L. A. Marley is a less confident and substantial image this time. She's brittle.'

'Brittle, eh? Then I should be able to smash her.'

Thomson smiled.

'It really is amazing, Franz, that Lou should prefer a crude and insensitive man, like yourself, to me, who understands her so much better. Your bulldozing tactics would only set up resistance and worsen the situation.'

'What do you advise, then? You're the mind-doctor.'

'For the time being, just humour L. A. Marley and ignore Lou hiding behind her. The hunted animal that's taken cover will never emerge while it knows it's being watched. But if it thinks no-one's giving it any attention, it'll begin to pluck up courage and poke its nose out again.'

'How long—'

'I knew you'd ask how long – the impatient always do. I can't tell you. Just practise patience, Franz – for once. Don't you think Lou's worth a little patience?'

Thomson was suddenly irritable. 'Hell,' he added, 'I've been patient, in my fashion, for years now. Waiting for passing time to heal either the wound or Lou. Foolish hopes, maybe, but they existed – until you popped up and blasted them. Well, blast you, too.'

'Sorry about that, Tommy. Not really my fault, though. I've never gone looking for women, least of all a *femme fatale*. It just happened. We're both in the same boat.'

'Oh, no, we're not. We're in separate boats. They're both holed, mine worse than yours, but, damn it, I'll bale that much harder. No more waiting around for miracles: one just gets shoved out of line.'

I stared at him. His was the anger of despair, and I realized that his kind of patience was ravelled close to breaking point.

'Oh, God!' he said, miserably, and closed his eyes and clasped his hand across them.

I walked out quietly. Back in my cabin I wondered how one set about learning patience. Relaxation seemed a likely first step, so I lay back in my chair trying to let the tension subside. There was plenty of it and it took quite a while.

But I did become calmer. My thought processes slowed, became more deliberate. Patience on a monument could smile at grief but I was on no monument and from where I sat could see nothing to smile at.

Why should Lou hide from me if she really loved me? There was no reason for her to be scared of me. Therefore, she was scared of the others. Again, of course, she was afraid of herself, of what she might have done unknowingly.

I must coax her out into life again. Small chance of success, though, while the others were around. Very well, then, I should take her far away from the others, from her father's grave and its disturbing memories, away from the ship altogether.

Just the two of us in the desert, isolated.

And I should be very patient with her.

Odd how things fell into place once you stopped trying to force them. For I could kill two birds with one stone this way.

I had known at the time that what L. A. Marley said about my duty to survey the Tycho streak was perfectly true. I could well imagine the reaction at the post mortem on my return if I skipped that task.

The chairman of the committee would raise his eyebrows.

'You have nothing to add to Miss Marley's report, Captain? You did not yourself go to the site and confirm these findings?'

I unrelaxed and reached for the phone.

X

THERE WAS NO REPLY FROM L. A. MARLEY'S CABIN. I RANG other likely places and remained unanswered. With a sigh, I set out on my flat feet.

I found her, together with Thomson and Pettigue, in the space-suit bay, all garbing themselves for a trip outside and almost ready to go.

I addressed them at large and with sarcasm: 'You're going places? Anyone care to tell me where?'

The usual unpregnant silence from Pettigue. The usual twisted smile from Thomson.

But from L. A. Marley: 'To no point further than a kilometre from the ship. I am ascertaining that nothing of importance has been overlooked within that radius. Hitherto, thanks to your negligence, Captain Brunel, prospecting has been desultory. But now I'm putting it on an organized basis. I shall sweep the northern semicircle and Mr Pettigue the southern. Later, we shall cover other regions, equally methodically.'

'You're planning a long stay, then?'

L. A. Marley judged this to be more sarcasm and not worth a reply. She continued fastening her suit, efficiently and without a fumble. Her icy beauty reminded me of the Princess Turandot.

I coughed politely. 'May I re-introduce myself? I'm Captain Brunel. The dictionary defines "Captain" as "the leader of a team". So that makes me the leader of this team. Now, Miss Marley, it so happens that I have different plans for you just now, so I'm afraid you'll have to postpone this little expedition of yours.'

'Indeed? What plans?' Each word came straight out of the refrigerator.

'I want you to take me to the spot where you found those sheets of... Marlionum.'

'Tycho's ray? You know perfectly well where it is, Captain. You don't need me to lead you by the hand. *You're* the leader: you just said so.'

'That's right, Captain: you just did,' said Thomson.

I didn't look at him, because I knew exactly what I'd see: the smile widened into a malicious grin.

'No, there's no point to my coming,' L. A. Marley continued, decisively. 'My time will be more usefully employed here.'

She snapped her final fastener with an eloquently final gesture which said, in mime: *'That* wraps up *that.'*

My automatic reaction was: 'Does it hell!' But that could shoot down my chances of contacting Lou again. So I swallowed my ire and found it tough stuff to digest.

I flung the undigested residue at Thomson: 'What precisely is *your* rôle in Miss Marley's scheme?'

'Me? Oh, I'm the fetch-and-carry man. In short, a porter. Miss Marley thinks I'm a natural for the job.'

'The trays of specimens are bound to become heavy, despite the one-sixth gravitation,' Miss Marley observed. 'It would be waste of time, energy, and Mr Pettigue's and my expertise to keep carrying them back to the ship. Therefore, we shall share Dr Thomson's services.'

Thomson, wryly and *sotto voce*, said: 'Waiter!'

'I see,' I said. What, in fact, I was seeing most clearly was the brick wall I'd walked into. 'Very well, carry on, Miss Marley.'

'Naturally.' Her tone was as cool and flat as the tundra.

Deflated, I wanted to hide. Move over, Lou, I'm coming in too. But I didn't really know where she was. However, there was the snug cave of my cabin and suddenly it became desirable.

I nodded distantly to L. A. Marley and walked out. As I climbed to my refuge, I tore a few strips off myself.

Admit it, Brunel: as the leader of the team you're a washout. Just because you dislike being ordered around there's no reason why you should also dislike ordering others around. All right, then, so you weren't born to the purple. You were happier as the loner you naturally are. Crews will always turn into myriad-headed monsters, devouring you crumb by crumb.

So never let yourself get into their clutches again. Get free and stay free.

Okay, you don't have to tell me: I could have bawled them all out. I could have overruled L. A. Marley and squashed her piddling beachcombing party. But at the same time I should have squashed Lou, too. It was all very difficult.

I gloomed awhile in my cabin, then decided I should have to go out to the Tycho ray alone. Well, that's what I want, isn't it – sweet solitude?

I radioed G.H.Q. and told them what was going on, but not why. They seemed happy with the idea that L. A. Marley had things well in hand. I signed off for another space.

Then I went down to the space-suit bay again. It was deserted now. I struggled into a suit and plodded – in the way you plod in these things – on to the garage.

A few minutes later I was inside the runabout and outside the ship. I was feeling a pretty lonely sort of loner. I stopped the runabout beside Marley's cairn and took a look around. This was difficult while wearing the helmet, so in a spasm of impatience

I took it off. I was getting tired of restrictions, of double precautions, of keeping to the book which everyone else seemed to have thrown out through the porthole. I wasn't a model skipper and would make no further pretence of being one.

Now I could see Pettigue in the distance, like a midge crawling across a bare and dreary expanse of concrete. There was a *real* loner. And a scared one, too, I guessed, in the midst of so much emptiness.

Way off in the opposite direction two figures, one behind the other, were progressing in slow, shallow leaps. L. A. Marley was leading – naturally – and Thomson trailing.

I called over the runabout's radio: 'Captain speaking. Are you receiving me? Answer in rotation: Marley, Thomson, Pettigue. Over.'

L. A. Marley snapped back: 'Loud and clear. Over.'

Thomson said: 'Ditto. Over.'

Pettigue came up with a little shake in his voice which confirmed my guess: 'Receiving you okay. Over.'

'Good,' I said. 'I'm proceeding to the north-eastern horizon where I shall set up a relay beacon and call you again. Off.'

I duly proceeded, using as an aiming point the mound where I had picked up the Colonel and Lou. As I passed its desolate slopes I remembered how they had sat there, happy and excited, only a short while ago. And now they had both departed this life...

I pressed on towards an empty horizon. It seemed a symbolic journey.

Suddenly, up spoke L. A. Marley – Miss Perkins to the life: 'Do you observe any eyes in the back of my head, Thomson? No? Then put the tray here, where I can see it.'

'Yes, ma'm. Sorry, ma'm.' The mock humility was overdone. It was a downright sneer.

There followed a longish silence.

Then, L. A. Marley again: 'That will do for the first load. Take it back to the ship. Don't waste any time. We're behind schedule now.'

'Don't waste time? The whole bloody idea's a waste of time. Any fool can see that all this area's the same kind of rock. I might as well be humping buckets of sand around the Sahara.'

Obviously her peremptory manner had nettled Thomson.

'Doctor Thomson—' She paused, and Thomson leaped in.

'Thanks for remembering I have a name and a profession, Miss Marley. I was beginning to think I was some kind of coolie.'

'It's edifying to learn that you are beginning to think about anything at all, Doctor Thomson. I must admit that any evidence of intelligence had previously escaped my notice.'

'*Who the hell do you think you are?*'

Thomson's grip on his temper had slipped and his mood had become ugly.

I almost butted in there but had second thoughts: I would try to remain neutral.

'I know very well who I am, Thomson. Please stop wasting time and take that tray back.'

'So you know who you are, do you? You think L. A. Marley is *someone*? That cerebrum on stilts? My ex-wife – that's a laugh: it was like being married to a computer. But you're not even L. A. Marley any more. Only a Hallowe'en mask, a hollow turnip-head—'

This was dangerous, so I butted in. I couldn't stop him talking but I could partially blot him out by my own transmission.

'Shut up, Thomson. Control yourself. Control yourself.'

I said it over and over again, loudly, until I judged he'd said his piece. I switched back to Receive. There was only the etheric wash.

I said: 'Now, listen to me, Thomson. Don't say another word to Miss Marley. Just stay quiet and take that tray back. Understood? Over.'

After a pause, he replied, strainedly: 'Understood. Wilco. Out.'

I had reached the lip of the ship's horizon by now, so stopped the runabout. I sat there for a short while, listening, but the radio remained silent.

If this had happened earlier, I should have turned back to sort out Thomson. I knew he was hovering perilously near to a crack-up. But having come so far, I might as well go on.

I donned my helmet, picked up a relay beacon, and went out through the airlock. I chose a spot for the beacon, unfolded its collapsible legs and set it up, sighting on the distant ship. Then I switched it on and inspected the meter dials. So far from giving a correct reading, all three of the needles remained at zero. I swore, and checked the connections. They all seemed to be okay.

So where was the fault? There was a set series of trouble-shooting tests for this kind of thing. Probably it would be quicker to dismantle the beacon, haul it back into the runabout, and either run through the tests there or choose another instrument. But I didn't like using the airlock more than necessary. Every time you came out you lost a lockful of air, and it was precious stuff.

Therefore, with my clumsy gauntlets, I fumbled through the tests, squinting through my face-plate. And found at length that the battery was a dud and I'd have to re-enter the vehicle for another, anyhow.

Wearily, I clambered back in, found a spare battery, and wisely tested it before going out there again. I connected it. The needles swung nimbly. Fine. I left it there.

Then back into the runabout. I drove on for almost a kilo: these beacons were best given the final test from a distance.

The runabout's radio was still receiving but I was deaf to it: I was still wearing my helmet and hadn't thought to switch on the suit's built-in set. Nor did I trouble to now. I removed my helmet and reached to transmit on the vehicle set.

My gloved fingers froze on the switch, for Thomson's fear-stricken voice shrieked from the speaker: 'God – no! *No!* Hel—'

There was an odd sound, like a door slamming. Then silence. I jabbed the switch down.

'Captain calling Thomson. What's wrong? Over.'

No answer.

'Captain calling Thomson. Can you hear me? Over.'

My instruments told me I was transmitting all right. I could only hope that the beacon was also doing its job. But, in case it wasn't, I turned the runabout in its tracks and drove back at top speed – which is considerably less than lightning: runabouts weren't designed for the Indianapolis.

Thomson remained dumb. So I tried: 'Captain calling Miss Marley. What's happening? Over.'

She replied at once, coolly and calmly: 'I don't know. Thomson set off back with the tray. He had almost reached the ship when I last saw him. I can't see him now. Possibly he is inside the ship. I am on my way back to investigate. Over.'

'Thanks. Keep me posted. Captain calling Pettigue. Do you know what's happened to Thomson? Over.'

There was no response. I called him again and again. Then I tried again to contact Thomson. But I seemed to be talking only to myself.

I had re-passed the beacon now and was rolling on towards the ship – it looked like a far-off church spire on the plain.

'Captain to Miss Marley. Can you see Pettigue anywhere? Over.'

She answered, measuredly: 'No, I can't, but I can see Thomson now. He is lying beside my father's grave, quite still. It looks as though he has collapsed or had some kind of accident. I shall report again when I reach him. Over.'

I acknowledged, then called Pettigue again, fruitlessly. I strained to see the area around the ship. The double distortion of face-plate and the runabout's windscreen (for want of a better description) combined with distance robbed the view of small detail. I could discern no movement there.

Pretty soon, L. A. Marley reported, without emotion: 'Doctor Thomson is dead. His face-plate is smashed. Over.'

I was too stunned to make an immediate reply. While I remained tongue-tied, the elusive detail came into focus at last. There was the cairn marking Marley's grave, with one tiny upright space-suited figure beside it and another lying full-length.

And then, from behind the cairn, another space-suited figure emerged: it could only be Pettigue.

I yelped over the radio: 'Pettigue! Where the devil have you been? Why didn't you answer my calls? Over.'

That effort merely added another unanswered call to the list.

Then I saw L. A. Marley go up to Pettigue and reach a hand to his chest – presumably to the switch panel there.

She said in my ear: 'Mr Pettigue had his radio switched off. It is on now.'

Pettigue, faintly stammering, said: 'I'm sorry, Captain. An oversight – I became absorbed in my work. I forgot I was off.'

'We'll discuss that lapse later,' I said, curtly, for I was nearing them now and the still form flat on the ground was engulfing my unwilling attention.

I drew alongside the cairn and got out. I looked down at Thomson. He lay on his back. His face-plate was shattered. So was his face.

There was a scattering of clearplast shards around him. I picked up and examined a couple.

Then, feeling sick, I looked more closely at his mutilated face. Something had drastically wiped the smile from it. The vacuum had caused the blood to boil through the exposed skin surfaces. A swift and ugly death which had expunged all personality. Thomson was gone, and there was left merely a mess.

I circled slowly around, seeking some trace of the object which had done this to him. There were only a few loose pieces of rock, none of them large enough to have caused this amount of damage. I peered into all the neighbouring small pits but harvested nothing.

I noted two specimen trays, heaped with samples, laid like offerings at the foot of the cairn.

I studied the cairn itself. There were several large chunks on it which I reckoned *could* have smashed a face-plate if hurled hard enough. But if one had been so used, then it had been neatly replaced.

By whom?

I glanced sidelong at the other two. They stood statue-still, watching me. I noticed that while Pettigue's electric rock-drill, together with his geologist's hammer, was hanging from his belt, L. A. Marley carried a hammer only.

I tapped the empty loop and asked: 'Where's your drill, Miss Marley?'

'I left it at the digging – which is about five hundred metres back that way. Why do you ask, Captain?'

'Just idle curiosity.'

A bit more of this idle curiosity remained to be satisfied. I set my teeth, turned Thomson on to his side, and examined the back of him.

Nobody commented, not even me.

I motioned the watching pair into the ship. We exchanged not a word while we waited in the airlock for the cycling to end. We removed our helmets and I shepherded my companions to the lounge.

I never felt more like using a stiff scotch, but there was none.

I commanded: 'Sit down and listen to me.'

They sat, with a yard of space between them.

'All right,' I said, 'I heard Tommy's last call. He exclaimed, "No!" Twice. With horror. And then a word which might have been "hell" or "help" cut short. What he might have said before that, I don't know: I had trouble with the relay beacon and was out of the communication for a while. So, what did he say prior to that?'

'Nothing of importance,' said L. A. Marley, tonelessly. 'Nothing in the least connected with his last strange call. Indeed, he had been silent for some time. Personally, I think he was merely swearing. "Hell" was a favourite expletive of his.'

I looked at her. Did she really believe that? Could she really be so insensitive as to be deaf to the terror in Thomson's voice?

'In my opinion, Miss Marley, that was the cry of a man in dire fear for his life. He was calling for help. But something hit him so suddenly that he couldn't finish the word. Don't you agree, Pettigue?'

But he didn't fall into my little trap. Maybe because he didn't know it was a trap… or maybe because he did. He looked away from me. However, that, for Pettigue, was usual. A flush appeared on his sallow cheeks. And that, for Pettigue, was unusual.

It might have been shame.

He mumbled: 'Sorry, Captain, but I didn't hear him. My radio was off.'

'Why? It was on when you started out. You answered my netting signal.'

'Yes, but – I switched off later.'

'Care to tell me why?'

He stuck out his lower lip but did nothing more with it. He was hinting that he didn't care to tell me why.

'You're refusing to answer?'

He refused to answer even that one.

So I turned back to L. A. Marley. 'All right, then let's hear your story.'

I had heard of black ice but never seen any. I saw some now: her eyes were made of it. She looked at me as though I'd made an indecent suggestion. Her mouth was prim.

'Please don't address me in the manner of some uncouth police chief. You're not the police and this isn't a murder case. Mr Pettigue and I are not on trial. We don't have to produce alibis or what you term a "story".'

'Not murder, Miss Marley? Then how would you describe it?'

'Accidental death, obviously. Doctor Thomson was unfortunate enough to be hit by a meteorite. That's a hazard we all accepted long ago.'

I shook my head. 'A small meteorite would have drilled a hole through the clearplast, not smashed it completely. Certainly it wouldn't have mutilated Thomson's face in that way. A larger meteorite could have done so, granted. But it would also have smashed right through his skull and out through the back of his helmet. You know the velocity of those things? Anything up to four miles a second.'

She replied with a silence I took to be consent.

'I emphasize that velocity,' I continued, 'because no human being could hope to glimpse a meteorite approaching him head on – or from any angle, come to that. It would be travelling faster than any bullet. But Thomson *saw* what was about to hit him. He cried out in panic. That clinches the fact that it was no meteorite.'

'Very well, if it wasn't a meteorite, what was it?' she asked.

I rubbed my chin.

'We-ll now, we're not alone on the moon, you know. Remember, too, that we're in a forbidden area. Also that we've discovered what might prove to be an enormously valuable mineral supply. Maybe we're being warned off, covertly, by agents of one of the less friendly Powers.'

'But – how? We've seen no-one but ourselves.'

'Suppose they parked their runabout hull down somewhere out there close to the horizon and observed us telescopically. Suppose they carried a guided missile launcher. And that they picked off poor Tommy. He *could* have glimpsed a guided missile homing on him.'

L. A. Marley nodded. 'That is a feasible explanation. And if they were able to recall their missile after impact, it also explains why there is no visible evidence of what hit Thomson.'

So far as she was capable of displaying human feelings, she seemed eager to accept this melodramatic fancy.

I said: 'There's just one thing, though. It does nothing to explain how your father died.'

Just as she had seemed about to loosen up a fraction, this observation froze her again. Her face went like stone. I could see that from now on she would be about as chatty as the Venus de

Milo. Even Pettigue would be an easier proposition, so I told him: 'I should like to see you in my cabin.'

He nodded, without exactly dislocating his neck.

I indicated that he was to precede me. He caught on. As we walked away I glanced back at L. A. Marley. She didn't see us go. She wasn't looking at anything in the world of here and now.

Up in the cabin, I said: 'Now, let's get to the bottom of this radio silence. I got the impression that you switched off because something was coming through that was painful for you to hear. And that it would be equally painful for you to repeat it in the presence of Miss Marley. Am I right?'

He launched another slight but successful nod.

'Would you object to repeating it to me?'

Yet another nod.

'Look,' I said, seriously, 'as Miss Marley observed, I'm not the police. But, as I see it, sooner or later you'll have to tell the police. Your holding out on me now isn't going to make it look any better for you then. You *do* realize you're under suspicion of murder?'

'What?' he said, feebly.

'Murder. Maybe double murder.'

He was aghast – or appeared to be.

'That's ridiculous, Captain. I'm the last man in the world capable of such a crime.'

'Then stop playing the oyster and tell me what you know.'

He hesitated. I waited. He hesitated some more and I became impatient.

'All right,' I said, 'I'll make a guess. After that spat with Miss Marley, which I stopped, Doctor Thomson diverted his spleen on to you. He began harping on that old Mato Grosso theme again. And you were doubly embarrassed, because you knew that Miss

Marley would be hearing those imputations, too, on her set. And you imagined I was, also, though in fact I wasn't. You just couldn't take it, and so—'

'No,' he interrupted. 'No, you're quite wrong. It was nothing like that.'

'No? Tell me this, then. What made you return to the ship so that you would reach it around the same time that Thomson would make it?'

'I wasn't thinking of Thomson or where he was. My tray was full. I was carrying it back.'

'Why? You knew that Thomson had been detailed for that duty.'

Pettigue looked hunted.

'Well, frankly, I didn't like to ask him. I was aware that he resented being used as a pack-mule. Also, he was in a very upset state. He would have told me to go to the devil.'

'What had upset him?'

'I really don't know, Captain. It was as if he had been brooding upon something for a long time, keeping it bottled up. And then suddenly it burst out. He began raving.'

'About what?'

'His feelings towards Miss Marley. He kept crying: "Lou, come back to me. Don't hide from me any more." Things like that. He was almost incoherent.'

'What was Miss Marley's reaction?' I asked.

'At first she kept telling him to be quiet. She sounded cold and stern. Then gradually she seemed to become affected by his intensity, and then became very angry. She shouted at him.'

L. A. Marley shouting? I tried to picture her that way. The vision remained obscure.

'What was she shouting, Pet?'

'That she didn't know anything about Lou. That there was no such person as Lou. And then she became confused. She started sobbing, repeating that Lou was wicked and had been sent to prison and would never be set free. Doctor Thomson said he would set her free. Then Miss Marley started crying: "Leave me alone! Leave me alone!" Over and over again. It was then that I switched off. Naturally, I felt embarrassed by having to listen to something so very personal to them and which didn't concern me. Apart from that, they were harrowing my nerves. After that, I concentrated on my digging and came upon some rather interesting formations and didn't think to switch on again.'

It all rang true enough. Pettigue couldn't possibly have invented that hysterical duologue.

I said: 'Yes, I can understand how you felt, Pet. Tell me, did you notice where Miss Marley happened to be at the moment when Thomson was struck?'

'No. I didn't even know when that moment was.'

'Of course, of course, your radio was off.'

'Apart from that, Captain, her digging and mine were on dia-metrically opposite sides of the ship. Therefore, the ship would block my view, anyway. And hers, of course. I didn't know that she had returned to the ship until I went past the cairn and saw her and Doctor Thomson there.'

I chewed on that and a fingernail for a while. If what he said were true, then he didn't, after all, arrive at the ship at the same time as Thomson but a fair time after the Doctor was dead.

Then: 'Right, thank you, Pet. I didn't know you had it in you to be so explicit. It's one hell of a situation. I don't know how I'm going to break the news to them back at G.H.Q. This has grown into a really classic case of a disastrous expedition.'

'I'm the Jonah,' said Pettigue, softly, unhappily. 'Every expedition I join ends in disaster. This is the last one. If I ever get back alive, I shall retire.'

I gnawed some more nail, regarding him.

'Do you have any reason to suppose you may not get back alive, Pet?'

'Well, when you consider that two of us have been killed violently and mysteriously, in so short a space, there seems no reason to assume that that's the end of it. I don't know what's behind these events, but I'm very frightened of it. I can't help it, although I try to: the fact remains that by nature I'm neither courageous nor optimistic. Any one of us may be struck down next.'

I was reminded of Thomson himself saying much the same.

'Any one of us – except the murderer,' I amended for him.

He turned away, and I saw him shiver.

XI

THE TWO UNPLEASANT TASKS WERE DONE.

I had reported Thomson's death. And we had buried him.

The dismay and confusion at Space Service G.H.Q. were deep and wide. I had to give the chiefs time both to absorb and confer on the facts. (The facts were of my selection: I didn't include L. A. Marley's radio performance, but I did mention that Thomson had seemed overwrought.)

The interment was carried out during the interval between the calling of the conference and the transmission of its conclusions.

I can't say that I had come to like Thomson, precisely, before the end. But I had come to feel sorry for him and (maybe because I was prone to feel sorry for myself) to regard him as a kind of fellow-sufferer: we both had Lou trouble. Anyhow, I felt no inclination to dance at his funeral.

If Pettigue did, he conquered the impulse. He appeared quite unmoved.

L. A. Marley showed some concern, though, about her ex-husband. She was concerned that he shouldn't be buried anywhere near her father and so spoil the splendid isolation of the great man's monument.

She talked as though we were burying a dog.

And she waited impatiently as I stumbled through the service: she was studying the properties of Marlionum and was anxious to get back to work. Pettigue had mentioned something to her about his study of the stuff, and this had persuaded her to resume their joint examination and postpone further prospecting in the area.

Thomson's shroud was his space-suit. Unlike as in the Marley case, there was small point to taking it back as an exhibit. A pulverized face-plate was a pulverized face-plate: that was all there was to it.

L. A. Marley, who seemed to have the pyramids of Cairo in mind, held that Thomson's memorial cairn should not, out of respect, be so high as Colonel Marley's, but rather be like the Second Pyramid in relation to Cheops'.

I had to remind myself that L. A. Marley was only an embodied symptom of mental illness and not responsible for all she said. All the same, this idiocy was hard for me to take.

I limited myself to a single comment: 'As the man said, death levels all things.'

And – minus feminine help – built Thomson's pyramid every bit as tall as Marley's.

G.H.Q. came through, at last, with the results of their deliberations.

First, I was censured for poor judgment, for lack of control over my crew, and for my carelessness in letting them get killed, maybe murdered.

I passed the buck back like a hand grenade.

I replied that *they* had selected, or at least condoned the choice of, my ill-assorted and wilful crew. That *they* had selected me also: I certainly hadn't volunteered. That the causes of the deaths were still unknown, but if they had any solutions to offer they would be preferable to blind censure.

Second, I was ordered to confine Pettigue and Miss Marley to their cabins – for their own safety, they added ambiguously.

'What do you mean by "confine"?' I asked.

Lock them in, they said.

I was reminded that Thomson had once advised me to lock Pettigue in his cabin. Even I didn't think to point out at the time that this was impossible. We tend to assume usual conditions and not notice what's under our noses.

I told G.H.Q. that if they cared to acquaint themselves with the plans of their ship, they would see that Miss Marley's cabin was the only room on board which had been fitted with a lock – presumably for her own safety, I added, sardonically and with lamentable taste.

Oh, they said.

'Shall I lock them both in Miss Marley's cabin?' I pursued.

No, they said.

'Then which of them shall I lock up?'

'That must be left to your own judgment, Captain.'

'But you've just told me that my judgment is poor.'

Do as you're told, they said. And, by the way, they added, wrap up the expedition and return to Earth as soon as you can. Too bad that you let things get out of hand after you reached the moon. But, at least, you did reach it and so prove that the future lies with atomic space-ships like the *Endeavour*. It showed that we could still lead the world.

'Thank you, gentlemen. You've made me feel proud and happy, and more than a little suspicious,' I said, and signed off.

I suspected they wanted to coax me back to London and give me a fair trial. Maybe the time had come for me to don my deerstalker cap and try to track down some kind of evidence which pointed in a direction definitely away from me. I didn't dwell on any fancies about which direction that might turn out to be.

I took a spare helmet from the space-suit bay out to the spot where Thomson had died. Then I began experimenting.

I set the helmet on the ground and lifted a large piece of rock from Marley's cairn. On Earth, I should have strained over its dead weight. Here, it was but a fraction of that weight. Either L. A. Marley or little Pettigue could have lifted it quite easily.

I raised it above my head with both hands, then hurled it with all my strength at the helmet's face-plate. My aim was pretty good. The rock smashed silently against the plate, dropped, and lay still.

It had remained intact. So had the face-plate.

Clearplast was tough stuff, all right. If I were to repeat this test on Earth, with the rock's weight increased six-fold, the face-plate would still survive. For it would, in effect, be an identical test. The weight ratio was irrelevant: it was the *inertia* of the rock which counted, the force of impact. And the inertia, which caused the damage, would be the same on Earth as on its satellite.

Just to clinch it, I tried again a few times with other rocks thrown from different angles. Never a crack appeared in the clearplast.

Right: it hadn't been done that way.

I had brought with me a geologist's hammer similar to the type carried by Pettigue and L. A. Marley. It wasn't all that big, of course, but there was a chance that, if swung ferociously, it would break the face-plate.

But again clearplast withstood my attack. And while no-one was likely to mistake me for Hercules, I doubted if my muscles were punier than those of my brace of suspects.

Correction: brace of former suspects.

For I could not see how either could have killed Thomson: the only weapons they had to hand were proven ineffectual.

Where did Sherlock Holmes go from here?

I gazed literally into space, the illimitable reaches of it beyond the horizon. At that moment it looked an inviting sort of place to go and get lost in. For I didn't relish going back to Earth to face the music. Not so much for my sake, as for Lou's. The pro 'tecs there might find a way to pin murder on her where I had failed.

If they did, the verdict could only be 'Guilty but insane'.

And that would end any hope of Lou returning to me and of our sharing our lives.

For a few mad moments, I considered kidnapping her, turning my back on Earth and driving the *Endeavour* onward, seeking an improbable sanctuary in some corner of the solar system. If we survived, we should be beyond the reach of the law for many years: there was only one *Endeavour*.

Pettigue would be a complication, though. Maybe if we took him along, we could train him to be our butler. On the other hand, if I could prove that he was the killer, it wouldn't matter: we could just leave him behind.

This nonsense streaming through my mind was the product of defeat and despair. Neither I nor anyone else was getting anywhere. L. A. Marley remained L. A. Marley. Pettigue remained an enigma. And Colonel Marley and Dr Thomson remained dead – and I still didn't know the reason why.

I pulled myself together and examined that obstinate face-plate again. So far as I could see, it wasn't even scratched. I reflected that it would take a pneumatic drill to break through it.

Drill! My thoughts froze on the word, then moved slowly on.

When I had caught up with the pair beside Thomson's body, Pettigue was carrying a drill but L. A. Marley was not: she said she'd left hers back at her digging.

Those drills packed a lot of power. They derived it from the new-type Pyke battery – a super job, fitted into the handle. The drill itself didn't rotate: it vibrated at a terrific rate, battering its way through material.

It could very well be the murder weapon in the Thomson case.

So far as I knew, L. A. Marley hadn't returned to that spot where she had been prospecting. Since I questioned her, there had been only one occasion on which she'd been outside the ship: her reluctant attendance of Thomson's burial.

She seemed to have lost interest in her original survey plan – maybe because there was no fetch-and-carry man now. Instead, she and Pettigue had become absorbed in further work on Marlionum in the lab.

I left the helmet lying there and walked out to her abandoned digging. Sure enough, a drill lay there at the edge of it. Her statement looked to be true.

I picked up the drill and went back. I knelt by the helmet and levelled the drill. At which moment, a movement caught my eye. The door of the ship's secondary airlock was opening.

Then, down the ladder, stepping precisely, came the space-suited figure of L. A. Marley. I stayed my hand, watched, and again wondered how Lou projected sex through a space-suit and why L. A. Marley signally failed to.

Maybe it was merely a matter of intention.

She came and stood over me, like a critical foreman.

'Exactly what are you doing here, Captain Brunel?'

Her voice was like having icicles stuck into my ears.

'Exactly what are *you* doing here, Miss Marley? I thought your research on Marlionum was highly important and pressing.'

'So it is. But we have treated all the sheets now, except one, which Mr Pettigue is still working on. We need to re-stock – urgently.'

'Sorry, but I'm fresh out of Marlionum.'

'Is that totally senseless observation intended to be humour, Captain?'

'It's no more senseless than your making a personal appearance to tell me you're out of Marlionum. You could have contacted me by radio more easily from the ship, Miss Marley.'

I was attempting to disconcert her, to fracture that glacial composure. I guessed she'd witnessed my rock-throwing experiments: the porthole of the lab. overlooked this spot. Why had she hastened out to investigate? L. A. Marley wasn't given to idle curiosity. She must have some motive.

Was she afraid I might stumble on the murder method? Was she therefore trying to divert my attention and head me away to the Marlionum deposit?

She said, expressionlessly: 'There is no need for me to tell you anything nor to request anything from you. As a matter of fact, I was on my way to get the Marlionum myself and pick up my rock drill *en route*. But I see that you have already collected the drill. Please return it to me.'

She held out her gauntletted hand.

The old, uneasy suspicions came creeping back just when I was beginning to dispel them. And the old sickness of heart came with them.

'Presently,' I said. 'Look, Miss Marley, I regret it but I'm having difficulty in believing you. Why should you walk all that way when the runabout is available? Remember, you found that walk more than a little exhausting the last time. Don't tell me you're just observing the old tradition of making the trail on foot. The trail has already been broken. Besides, you say the replenishment is needed urgently. So why waste all that time? It's not like you to waste time, Miss Marley.'

Her hand dropped to her side and she made no reply. At last I'd breached her defences, but I wasn't cheering myself because of it.

'You wanted to know what I'm doing here,' I went on. 'Very well, I'll show you.'

I started the drill and applied it to the face-plate of the spare helmet. I've forgotten how many times the point of that drill vibrated per second, but a mere three seconds' worth of vibrations were sufficient. The plate first starred, then split into sharp shards which fell away.

I got slowly to my feet, seeing a vision. There's Pettigue, goaded at last by Thomson's malice to the point of frenzy, waiting behind the cairn. As Thomson reaches it, he steps out and lunges with his deadly drill. Thomson barely has time to cry out, then it's over. Pettigue, still possessed by maniacal fury, smashes at his persecutor's face, either with the drill or his hammer.

He is avenged. He is a man who has proved to himself that he can hit back at the bully and even destroy him.

Pettigue, I knew, had a desperate need to prove something of the kind.

I looked at L. A. Marley. She was certainly disconcerted now. Indeed she seemed dazed. I couldn't guess what was passing through her mind and I didn't ask. Any comments just now could be dangerous, for they would be broadcast. While there was no radio in the lab., Pettigue could have been watching me from there and gone along to the signals room to eavesdrop. Therefore, I must be cautious.

'Let's go back in now, Miss Marley. We'll go into the Marlionum question with Pettigue. Then, if I judge the need absolutely necessary, I'll take the runabout out to the deposit.'

Still unnaturally quiet and subdued, she followed me into the ship.

Pettigue was in the lab. Maybe he'd been there all the time. Maybe he'd just stolen back there. Anyhow, there he was peering through a binocular microscope at a shred of Marlionum with a convincing appearance of concentration.

'Pettigue,' I said, and he started.

He looked up at us. 'Oh… Yes, Captain?'

'Miss Marley tells me that you want some more of that stuff. When I discussed it with you once before, you didn't seem to think it of much value.'

'I think I said it had no obvious monetary value, Captain. I had no reason then to suspect it had any particular value, scientifically speaking, either, except that its unusual structure might contribute something to atomics. But the more Miss Marley and I have examined it, the more we're persuaded that this structure contains something analogous to the organic pattern Miss Marley had detected in certain carbonaceous meteorites.'

'That's important?'

He nodded.

'Very. Its implications are tremendous. It's vital that we take back with us a fresh supply of this element – virgin sheets, as it were – for thorough examination in properly equipped laboratories. This small one has obvious limitations. We just haven't the tools. We're groping, and our guesses can't be verified. One needs an electron-microscope, for one thing.'

Miss Marley added nothing to this. She was watching me, not Pettigue. Her eyes held unspoken questions and it seemed to me that I caught a fugitive glimpse of the early, troubled Lou in them. Or maybe I was just making myself see what I was looking for.

I said to Pettigue: 'You've gone about as far as you can go, then?'

'I'm afraid so.'

'It's just as well,' I said, 'for you won't be able to do any further work in here, anyway. I'm sorry, Pet, but G.H.Q. has ordered me to confine you to your cabin. Which in practice means you'll have to change cabins with Miss Marley, since hers has a lock.'

This time I was sure Lou, startled, peeped from behind the mask. But L. A. Marley still held her tongue.

Pettigue didn't. He burst out: 'This is plain damn silly, you know. What grounds did they give?'

I shrugged. 'What does it matter? I have to do it, and you'll have to accept it. The arguing of whys and wherefores can only be done back at G.H.Q. So let it wait. Miss Marley, would you mind removing your personal belongings from your cabin and transferring them to Mr Pettigue's?'

She went without a word.

I said: 'The same, but in reverse, goes for you, Pet.'

'Don't call me "Pet",' he snapped, still angry. 'You're no friend of mine. For a time you fooled me… I thought you weren't wholly unsympathetic. I began to trust you. But, obviously, you were only angling for confidences and trying to trip me up. G.H.Q. would never have issued an order like that if you hadn't persuaded them to: they know nothing but what you've reported to them. Heaven knows what nonsense you've told them, but this time I'm not taking it lying down. I'll not have any more mud flung at my name. You're no better than Thomson – in fact, worse. At least he accused me to my face.'

I said: 'I haven't accused you and I'm not accusing you. I have reasons why I must play it safe: I can't risk any more killings. My reasons may turn out to be ill-founded. Believe me, I hope they do. I hope like hell you clear yourself. But in the circumstances, I have no choice.'

He stared at me. A straight, hard stare, the first of its kind I had seen from him.

'Lock me up, then, if you must, Captain. But let me assure you of one thing: *the killer will still be at large.*'

He turned and walked out. I gazed bemusedly at the empty doorway for a few moments, then anxiously hurried after him.

Pettigue settled in. I left a radio with him.

'This is so that you won't feel entirely cut off from us,' I explained, but didn't explain further that it was also because I didn't want to be cut off from him on the occasions when I had to leave the ship. One such occasion was already imminent.

It was one way of keeping tabs on him to some extent.

His response was to turn his back on me.

I locked the door on him, checked that it was indeed firmly locked and stuck the key in my pocket. Then I went along to his old cabin. L. A. Marley was still arranging her things in there in a listless kind of way.

I said: 'I'd like you to come with me to Tycho ray, if you will, and help collect a new batch of those sheets. I think you said they're fairly easy to detach from the parent stream?'

'Did I?'

I hesitated. I recalled now that it was Lou who'd said that, not L. A. Marley. I decided not to debate the point.

'I should appreciate your assistance, anyhow.'

She acknowledged with a slight nod, but made no move. It was as though she were waiting for something else. I guessed what it might be, but knew I must walk warily. Thomson had been right: the direct frontal approach could ruin everything.

I remarked casually: 'Did you see me chucking those rocks at that helmet and bashing its face-plate with a hammer?'

She nodded again.

'I couldn't make any impression on it.'

'But the drill did,' she observed, watching my face.

'Yes. Exactly. That's the chief reason I had to put Pettigue under restraint. He was the only person carrying a drill at the moment of Tommy's death.'

She gave a little sigh. There was both sadness and relief in it. She was sad because Pettigue, it seemed, had done such an awful thing; and relieved because this new evidence pointed to her innocence. I guessed that this was what she had been waiting for: reassurance about herself.

Impatience undid me. Rashly, I began: 'Lou, I understand—'

'Lou?' she frowned. 'Please, Captain, don't let us discuss Lou. She knows nothing about this affair and has no wish to become involved.'

Lou was present, all right, but only in the third person.

'Of course, Miss Marley. Let's go.'

For some time I had been playing with the idea of taking Lou right away from the ship area and its associations, and then circumspectly trying to re-establish contact with her.

And now here we were, riding side by side across the lonely Mare. Yet instead of thinking about her, I found it difficult to detach my attention from the ship.

I was uneasy about Pettigue. I hadn't liked the idea of leaving him alone in the *Endeavour*. Still, he was a prisoner and could not harm the ship.

Or could he? I tried to envisage ways by which he might sabotage it from inside his makeshift cell, but could imagine none. I had made quite sure there was nothing in the cabin he could use as a destructive implement – not even a self-destructive one.

Again, I realized that this line of thought was pre-judging him, and that no-one had the right to do that. A rock-drill *could* break a face-plate, but it didn't necessarily follow that Thomson's had been broken in that way, even though I could see no other way that it could have happened.

I kept remembering the way Pettigue had emphasized that the killer was still at large. Bluff?

If it were not, then he could be referring only to Lou. Did he really believe she was responsible? But she couldn't be. She'd left her drill behind at the digging, and had no other weapon.

I found myself wishing I'd checked *at the time* where she'd left that damned drill. Maybe, originally, it hadn't been so very far away. And then, later, she had slipped out of the ship without my knowing and planted it back at the digging to corroborate her story.

Maybe that.

Or maybe this – or, again, that.

I was losing myself in a welter of speculation. The few facts I'd established were insufficient to give a firm footing, and I hadn't a clue about where to look for more. This, I feared was another *Mystery of Edwin Drood,* destined to remain unfinished and unexplained. Maybe Dickens himself hadn't known who killed Drood. And maybe the author of these crimes didn't know who killed Marley and Thomson…

I stole a glance at L. A. Marley. The mask was still there. Of course, I saw only its surface. It could be as thin as paper or as thick as armour plating. Lou was behind it somewhere – but what kind of Lou? Timid and shrinking? Scared and desperate? Rebellious and angry?

Sane – or insane?

Belatedly, it occurred to me that this journey with her across the blank Mare might entail a peril deadlier than meteorites, dust-swamps, thin patches of crust, or the other natural hazards of the moon.

But surely, Lou loved me. And, sane or not, she would never—

But Lou had loved her father, too. Yet that love hadn't saved him.

Then, again, she had also hated him.

Maybe this intensely neurotic ambivalence was the core of the danger.

And now I began to hate myself for what I was surmising, for building a case with only straws for evidence. Because I despised my fear and suspicions, I changed my mind about having L. A. Marley set up the Automatic Relay Unit when we reached the horizon.

I clambered out and did it myself.

I felt I had to put the matter to the test, just to relieve the suspense. If I lost the gamble, then what the hell difference could it make? It would only confirm that I had lost Lou altogether in one way instead of another.

I deliberately prolonged my stay outside to give her every chance to slide into the driving seat and career back to the ship. Leaving me marooned – and a dead man, if she barred the ship to me after I'd walked back. For airlocks had doors which *could* be fastened.

The ARU beacon worked first time. I called Pettigue.

'Just checking. Are you all right?'

'That's a rather fatuous question, Captain.'

'Yes, I suppose it was, from your view-point. But I'm on a run-out to get your precious Marlionum, and it's just as well to keep in contact in case anything goes wrong out here.'

'Is Miss Marley with you?'

I hesitated. 'Yes.'

'What kind of mishap or calamity are you thinking of, Captain?'

Was I imagining the insinuation in his remark?

'The standard hazards: anything from a mechanical breakdown to a meteorite shower.'

'Well, telling *me* about it wouldn't help, would it? What could I do about anything? I couldn't even inform G.H.Q. You cage me like a rat and leave me to it. Suppose something *does* happen and you never come back. Have you thought of the consequences to me? I should starve slowly to death in here.'

'I'll try to be very careful,' I promised.

'Nevertheless, I'm glad it's you out there and not me. It may surprise you to learn that I wouldn't wish to change places with you, Captain. That emptiness terrifies me. Dr Thomson's diagnosis was correct: I have agoraphobia. When I brought my tray of specimens back to the ship it wasn't because it was all that full or because I had found anything particularly interesting. Those were excuses. The truth is that my nerve was cracking, being out there on my own. I had to have the feeling of *walls* around me protecting me from the vacuum. Well, I certainly have them now, thanks to you. So don't worry too much: so long as you return safely, I shan't be too unhappy.'

'I'm glad to hear it. I think I know how you feel, Pettigue. Teilhard de Chardin called it "immensity sickness".'

True, and as a matter of fact de Chardin also said that its victims had an intense desire to be important and responsible members of a community to compensate for their lack of roots. But the awareness of the emptiness under their feet was their cross. Whenever they saw emptiness, their response was fear.

Now the Space Age was increasing their insecurity. Its unlimited horizons, its moving outward into a universe too vast for comprehension, inspired them with panic. They became sick with apprehension.

Yet, otherwise, they desperately wanted to have a place in life, to be respected and to respect themselves.

So, in a way, Pettigue's imprisonment meant a respite from this conflict. No one could condemn him for taking shelter, for the condition wasn't of his making. And complete freedom entailed demands which strained his inadequate resources.

After realizing all this, I didn't feel so bad about what I'd done to the little man.

'An apt term,' Pettigue replied. 'However, don't let me detain you further. I'll leave the radio on, so call me any time you want. You know what, Captain? I suspect you understand my feelings because you share them – sometimes. The important difference is that you have, additionally, the supreme virtue: courage. And so you get by.'

'Nuts,' I said, tersely. 'Goodbye, now.'

All the same, it was a shrewd comment and not far off the mark. I think he overestimated my courage, though, and underestimated my talent as an actor.

The Pettigue worry shelved, if not settled, I turned my attention on L. A. Marley. As still as a fly in amber, she sat inside the clearplast bubble gazing to the next horizon without interest. She wasn't even interested in killing me, apparently. Nor, any longer, in getting to the so-important deposit of Marlionum.

I had left the radio working in the runabout. She must have heard my conversation with Pettigue. Had it persuaded her that Pettigue was no murderer, and therefore Lou was once more suspect?

Certainly, the brief flicker of Lou that I had detected – so I thought – had died completely. Self-hypnosis had resumed its sway, though with a difference: L. A. Marley wasn't confident and authoritative now. She was a frozen likeness, a waxwork, with nothing to say for herself.

I negotiated the airlock and resumed the driving seat. L. A. Marley remained as dumb as the Sphinx but without its ghost of a smile.

I drove on. Presently I saw, stretched along the horizon ahead, a bright line under the Earthlight. The Tycho streak.

As we neared it, the effect became spectacular. We were coming upon the bank of a frozen river of metal so wide that we couldn't see the other side. It appeared so effulgent to my eyes – accustomed to the dull rock-bed – that I was forced to shade them for a while.

I could imagine how the first sight of this golden splendour must have smitten Colonel Marley. Not just elusive specks in the riffles of his sluicing-box, this, but the sudden and overpowering spectacle of the shining towers of El Dorado itself.

It was strange that while, unlike he, I knew it wasn't gold at all, I yet felt a surge of excitement. Perhaps, at second-hand through Marley's daughter and Pettigue, I sensed that here was an abundance of something even more precious than gold.

I stopped the runabout a short distance from the verge.

Then I opened the airlock door and conveyed to L. A. Marley to go out first. She had been here before and knew the technique. When I followed her, she was already kneeling at the river's brim, peeling off a diamond-shaped sheet of Marlionum.

She held it up for a moment between her metallic gloves, studied it, and then spread it carefully beside her. She reached for another.

I gazed past her at the bright river under the bright stars. Marley must have stood here feeling like a king – Ruskin's *King of the Golden River* personified.

There were scores – doubtless, in the far flow, thousands – of thousands of these diamonds laid out neatly, slightly overlapping. They were like the scales of some enormous goldfish.

It was the strangest natural formation I had seen since the 40,000 truncated basaltic pillars, hexagonal or octagonal in section, of the Giant's Causeway, in Ireland.

I remarked as much to L. A. Marley.

She replied, witheringly: 'When you're through sightseeing, I should appreciate some assistance here.'

L. A. Marley was herself again, it seemed.

I assisted.

It was difficult to assess the texture of the stuff as it hung in the resistless void from one's stiff, encased fingers, but I got the impression that it was as floppy as wet cardboard. The sheets the Colonel had brought back seemed to me, retrospectively, somewhat stiffer. I thought it possible that their composition might vary from place to place.

Anyhow, between us we amassed a fair pile of them.

'Enough?' I asked, at length.

'Yes, this will suffice.'

We humped it into the airlock. Then I went in and dragged it through. I got to my seat and waited for her to join me. She seemed to be taking her time, if not dragging her heels. I glanced irritably at the driving mirror (it's a devil to turn, seated, in a suit) and saw her standing rock-still and apparently gazing into the distances to our left.

'What's keeping you, Miss Marley?'

'I saw something moving in the sky. I only glimpsed it. It seems to have gone now.'

'Gone where?'

'That's what I should like to know… There it is again.'

I turned quickly and stared at the star-sprinkled sky to my left. Something up there flashed briefly, like the wing of a banking aeroplane momentarily catching the sunlight. I waited maybe half a minute and didn't see it again.

'Get in now, Miss Marley – quickly, please.'

She obeyed without argument.

I swung the runabout away from the golden river while she was still in the airlock.

'Wait, Captain, don't leave yet,' she said, via radio.

'It may not be healthy to wait,' I said. 'That could be a guided missile up there and I'd rather be a moving target.'

'Didn't you see the shape of it? I did, that second time. It's a diamond. I'll swear it was a sheet of Marlionum.'

I slowed the runabout.

'You're sure?'

'Don't waste time with tiresome rhetorical questions, Captain. I said I'll swear to it.'

I stopped the runabout.

'Pettigue,' I called, 'are you getting this?'

'Yes, Captain. I have no explanation to offer, but if I were you I should waste no time in getting back here, under cover. Marlionum is very peculiar stuff. That's why we've become interested in it.'

'H'm. All the more reason, then, why it should be studied in its natural state, instead of being laid out cold on a laboratory slab. I'm going to cruise alongside the ray for a while, to see what we can see. Keep listening.'

'And you keep *watching*, Captain, in all directions.'

I drove on at a moderate speed, keeping one eye on the sky and the other on the shining expanse on our right. I debated about driving out across the ray itself for a distance, but Pettigue's caution underlined my own. We were literally skirting the edge of the unknown, and memories of how our party had been hit by the unknown lately curbed rashness.

'There's another... no, two of them. Gone now,' reported L. A. Marley, pointing to a quarter of the sky I wasn't regarding. 'They're definitely Marlionum sheets floating high above ground.'

'Can you estimate their height?'

'I should say around the hundred metre mark.'

'I accept that,' I said, 'though it's hard to credit. How can anything float in a vacuum?'

'Quite easily. Have you ever seen sheets of aluminium moving unsupported in the field of a giant electro-magnet? They could do so just as easily in a vacuum, I assure you, Captain.'

'You mean, electrical currents are keeping those detached sheets afloat up there?'

'Must you keep asking these rhetorical questions?'

'I don't know any other kind,' I said, lamely. 'Good heavens, look at that!'

I braked sharply, stabbing a finger at the latest portion of the Tycho ray to come into view.

The diamond shapes composing it were all on the move, drifting over each other like so many flat-fish on the sea-bottom. Now and again, some planed upwards and glided around in the void above – blank, featureless pterodactyls. I was groping mentally for metaphors: fish or flying reptiles, living things... or dead autumn leaves borne on the airless wind?

There was no floppiness about these specimens. They were as stiff as metal cut-outs sliced to conform to some diamond-shaped jig.

"'Like a tea-tray in the sky,'" L. A. Marley quoted softly.

Even at that time of astonishment, I glanced at her with further surprise. L. A. Marley was as dust-dry and humourless a person as, say, Charles Lutwidge Dodgson. But Dodgson was, in fact, a dual personality: he was also Lewis Carroll. And L. A. Marley was quoting Carroll.

This was, undoubtedly, Lou breaking free in an unguarded moment.

Just then, in her turn, she pointed to a spot on the no longer frozen river.

'Regardez!'

She was indicating one of the nearer diamonds which was far thicker than its neighbours. I began to wonder why, and then there was no further need to: I saw why. Taking it leisurely in turn, adjacent diamonds were sliding on top of it, covering the area exactly. It was as though they were sliding into place with an unheard click.

Each time, of course, they added their own slight thickness to the pile.

The process was smooth, continuous, and hypnotic to watch. Centimetre by centimetre, the pile became taller. The sheets composing it fitted so closely face to face that they weren't perceptible individually: the pile looked like a solid block.

I called Pettigue and gave him an eye-witness account of what was going on. I had a feeling that Pettigue somehow – despite his predicament – would survive, even if we didn't. As Thomson once remarked of him, he was a born survivor. And even if he failed on this occasion, he could yet compile a record which would survive for the benefit of those men who followed, eventually, the trail of the *Endeavour*.

I told him to write it down.

L. A. Marley was thoughtfully watching both the self-building block and the loose sheets which skimmed up into the sky, wheeled, vanished, reappeared, flashing intermittently in the Earthlight. They didn't vanish in actual fact, of course: it was merely an effect due to their turning edge-on to our line of sight. At that angle they were too thin to be visible at any distance.

Some of them began to dive and sweep past us at head level and shoot up again as though they were gulls inspecting us curiously but cautiously. I had the strange impression that they were indeed sentient creatures, and yet it seemed obvious that their general restlessness was aimless, a random motion.

I described this to Pettigue.

He asked: 'How thick is that block now?'

I sized it up. 'Around ten centimetres.'

'As much as that? That's a considerable mass of Marlionum.'

'We've collected about as much ourselves, in loose sheets. You want me to try for the block as well?'

'No, no, Captain, don't go out there. Supposing the block took off when you got to it.'

'You mean, supposing it took me off with it – like a magic carpet?'

'No. I mean if a mass like that flying around happened to crash into you—'

He broke off.

The implication of the possibility he was describing overtook me a second after it had silenced him.

'Good grief, did it happen like that to Tommy?' I exclaimed. 'I'll bet my last dollar it did, you know. He would have seen the thing coming. And then the sharp corner of the diamond smashing into his face-plate like a wedge… It would have done just that kind of damage. Yes, that's the way it was, I'm certain. Lord, Pet, I'm sorry I ever thought it was you or…'

I dried up, turning slowly to look at L. A. Marley.

She wasn't there. But Lou was. Her eyes were bright with sudden tears. (L. A. Marley wouldn't know how to weep.) She was attempting to smile. (L. A. Marley's prim, pursed mouth would never even have tried.)

'Or me?' she asked, softly.

I always found the encumbrance of space-suits frustrating and now more so than ever. Our helmets were off but still I couldn't reach her lips. I could do no more than put an arm around her, clumsily.

'I never really believed *that*, darling.'

I suppose I was lying. Even now, I'm not sure, one way or the other.

She said: 'Damn these silly gloves. I can't wipe my eyes.'

'Never mind. There'll be no more crying, after this. Where have you been, little lost lamb? God, I've missed you.'

'I don't know, Franz, I really don't. What happened to me? I've been so confused. Sometimes I seemed to know you and sometimes you were like a stranger. Have I been dreaming or delirious… or am I going insane?'

'It was just nervous exhaustion, dear. We've all been under severe strain, we've all been feeling it. There were times when I thought I was going out of my mind.'

'It began when that dreadful thing happened to Dad,' she said. 'I couldn't get over the shock. And I got to thinking and remembering too much. I was so afraid that I... oh, I couldn't bear it. But now I'm sure I know what really happened. Nobody was to blame. Nobody fixed that Marlionum sheet – in fact, it didn't come from the lab. at all. It was one – probably just one of many – sailing around like those out there. It got caught on the cooling control and tangled around it, and he couldn't free it. So he tried to get back to the ship. Poor Dad – it must have been awful.'

Strange how, for me, the Marley mystery had been largely overlaid by the more recent Thomson tragedy. But for Lou, naturally, it loomed over everything else. Considering it now, while watching those swooping diamond shapes, I concluded that Lou's explanation was almost certainly the truth.

Pettigue returned, apologetically: 'Excuse my interrupting, but I think this is important. From his position when found, I judge Colonel Marley's trouble happened some distance from the Tycho ray, even allowing for his attempt to get back to the ship. Again, that block which hit Dr Thomson – if our theory is correct – must have travelled all the way from the ray to the cairn. Evidently, the electro-magnetic field isn't confined to the locality of the ray. It must stretch all the way back here to the ship, at least. And all of it is a danger area. So you're not safe anywhere outside of the ship. Now, if that block you describe – or any other like it – starts moving within the field, you could be hit by it. Remember, your only shield is clearplast, which we know now can't stand up to that kind of impact.'

'You're right, of course, old man,' I said. 'We'll start back very soon. All the same, I think you're exaggerating the danger. There's an awful lot of space around, you know, and the chance of being hit is only comparable to the meteorite hazard.'

'Chance?' Pettigue echoed. 'Do you think that two men, at different times and in different places, were hit by mere chance? Imagine the chances *against* that happening! No, statistically, those hits were well above chance level.'

'You're not implying that the damn things killed the Colonel and Thomson deliberately? Hell, they're only lifeless pieces of metal.'

Even as I said that, I wondered, recalling my first impression of them.

'Miss Marley and I doubt that they're completely inert. As I told you, we detected traces of what could be organic structure. I don't say they have any kind of brain, any more than an amoeba has, but I suspect that they react in a primitive way to other objects – maybe just other metals or alloys – which impinge on the lines of that magnetic field. It's this triggered reaction we need to study: at the moment the only guess I can make about it is that it does exist.'

I looked questioningly at Lou, seeking confirmation. She was frowning.

She said, hesitantly: 'I think he's right, darling. I'm trying to remember, but I'm seeing through a fog. There *were* some tests in the lab… yes, I believe he's right. It's dangerous out here. Let's go.'

'Right,' I said, and started the engine.

As we moved off, we saw the thick block of Marlionum close by move also. It took off and glided smoothly up a path which would take it somewhere above our heads.

XII

'U H-HUH,' I SAID. 'DON'T LOOK NOW BUT I THINK WE'RE being followed.'

'That block?' asked Pettigue, anxiously.

'Yes. Lou, dear, put your helmet on.'

I reached for mine.

If our outer rampart, the plastic bubble, were breached, we should still have our suits as an inner defence. True, they weren't impervious, either, but they might gain us time to reach the ship.

The golden river receded behind us but not fast enough for my liking. The runabout was no winged chariot and allowed us plenty of time to take in the scenery: it was only doing its job, after all.

The block had reached a fair altitude now and looked small. It was weaving around a good deal but following generally in our wake. It was as though we were flying a kite as we bowled along, with the string attached to our rear bumper. It was thick enough to be visible edgewise and we never lost sight of it.

I wished like hell it would lose sight of us. But that was foolish: it had no eyes – only, probably, a vague awareness.

But if it had no eyes, it had the compensatory advantage of wings, or the equivalent thereof. Minute for minute, it travelled much further than we did. Only the fact that its course was tortuous and ours a bee-line kept it behind.

Though, of course, it might be playing cat and mouse.

Or, more aptly: *The Tortoise and the Hare*, I said. 'We're going flat out, Pettigue, but the thing has the heels of us. We're just hoping it'll lose interest and go away.'

'And play with its mates,' added Lou, pointing.

I looked up. At eleven o'clock high, five or six similar blocks were playing Ring-a-Ring-of-Roses. My heart sank to six o'clock low.

Just for good measure, there was a descending shower of loose golden leaves not far off, too, as if someone had emptied a waste-basket from a window in heaven.

My arm went around Lou again, and squeezed. Maybe her space-suit felt comforted, but little of the squeeze could have reached her.

'Watch it,' she said. 'That's dangerous driving.'

I was reassured: Lou was fully back with me. The old Lou, cool under fire and armed against peril with the ready crack. Most of the courage Pettigue mistakenly thought I had was confirming its absence, but Lou had plenty in reserve. Just to know it was there was like a shot in the arm to me.

I said, almost gaily: 'It's a shame there isn't more traffic on the roads to spread Mr Block's attention. Being the only pebble on the beach has its drawbacks.'

'I see you still mix a pretty good metaphor,' said Lou.

A couple of loose sheet-diamonds overtook us, performed a sort of love-dance way out in front of our windscreen, then shot apart.

'Boy mets girl, boy loses girl,' Lou commented.

Pettigue was in no joking mood, though. No doubt he'd been reflecting that being safe from bombardment in his cell promised a dim future if the only warder with the key was obliterated.

Anyhow, his voice shook a little as he asked: 'Can you see the ship yet, Captain?'

'We should do at any moment... Yes, there's my cabin just showing on the edge of the horizon.'

But it wasn't. The double clearplast diffraction and my own wishful thinking had fooled me. The brightish speck was, I then discerned, only a lone star.

However, shortly afterwards, the upper tip of the *Endeavour* did lift into view.

Although it still seemed to be stalking us, the block hadn't shown any marked enthusiasm for the chase or antagonism towards us. Its fellows were still circling merrily up there.

So much for appearances. Lou sang out, suddenly: 'Look out, below!'

Confused, I tried to look all ways, then glimpsed the block coming for us like a bomb. It was streaking down and across the star-curtain. A literally striking spectacle that I didn't dwell on. I spun the driving wheel hard left and nearly overturned the runabout.

This violent evasive action saved us. At just about the spot where we should have been if I hadn't taken it, the heavy diamond struck arrow-point foremost. Well-sprung though the runabout was, we felt the ground-shock.

The thing drove itself into the hard rock like a trowel going into soft earth. There it stuck, looking like an arty kind of gravestone – it was very nearly *our* gravestone.

'Yah – missed!' Lou crowed.

I didn't feel like crowing, nor yet trusting myself to speak. I could feel the acid flow starting along my stomach lining.

Pettigue sent an agitated inquiry but I didn't take in what he said. Lou answered with something comforting and untrue.

For we weren't out of the wood yet. One of the circling hawks above peeled off and went into a similar power-dive – in our direction.

This time I braked hard, dropping to a crawl. In consequence, the second diamond overshot us. It started to pull out of its dive too late and made a pancake landing. Its impetus carried it along, skipping like a flat stone across water in a game of Ducks and Drakes.

Way off on the Mare, it slithered to a stop and lay perfectly still.

'Broke its neck,' said Lou, complacently.

'It could be it's just shamming,' I said, and watched it warily until we were well past it.

Lou, doubtless more wisely, watched the remaining hawks.

The *Endeavour* was standing like a lighthouse on the waveless sea of rock. I kept the runabout's nose pointed to it and urged the sluggish vehicle on.

Once safe aboard, I would waste no time in taking off. My former reluctance to return to Earth was gone: the whole picture had changed. The loss of half my crew couldn't reasonably be laid at my door, not now. Lou, likewise, was cleared of blame – especially self-blame. My crime of landing in a forbidden area would, I anticipated, be overlooked in the light of the fantastic discovery we had made there: Marlionum would put the scientific world in a state of ferment.

And I had outgrown my fear of the sound of wedding bells.

All we had to do to gain absolution and garner the rewards was to survive for another five minutes.

One of the dashboard instruments was small but important. It was a radio transmitter, on a fixed wavelength, designed to send a signal to open the ship's garage door and lower the ramp automatically.

My finger was itching to push its button, but I knew I must hold back to the last moment. I didn't wish to risk that large door being wide open for a minute longer than was necessary: one of the diamonds could – and might – beat us to it. The thought of what damage the thing could cause on a rampage inside the ship made me shudder.

I never did push that button.

Lou said: 'Here comes another.'

'Damn the things!'

I looked for it, hating it. Down it was coming in a falcon's stoop. I tried to estimate its probable point of impact so as to miss the appointment. But this time it was an appointment in Samarra, destined, unavoidable.

For, as I started to steer away, a whole flock of loose Marlionum sheets swept straight into our windshield. Most of them skated back over the top of our bubble cabin and fell behind. But one caught against the radio aerial and folded around it, looking like a golden pennant.

More seriously, another plastered itself across the windscreen and blocked my view.

For a few seconds, partially blinded, I lost orientation and wavered.

And the thick diamond block hit us.

I had almost made it miss, but not quite. It smashed down through the airlock behind us, drove through the floor (breaking the driving shaft), and pinned the runabout by its tail to the solid rock.

The front of the vehicle was flung upwards. So were we. We thumped against the clearplast ceiling. Only our helmets saved us from splitting our skulls. The concussion near split our eardrums instead. I saw coloured lights, heard great brass bells clanging, and bit my tongue. My head was spinning.

The two large front wheels were spinning too, but well clear of the ground – getting nowhere. The now driveless back pair were, I noticed later, looking knock-kneed. The rear axle was broken.

The airlock roof was, of course, stove in. A fissure ran from the hole and crossed the cabin ceiling we'd just rebounded from. From outside the bubble must have looked like a split grape.

The split was narrow – a mere finger-width or two – but all the air in the cabin had already departed through it: the pressure gauge stood at zero.

So our outer rampart was breached, after all, and our suits had saved us from suffocation. But for how long?

My head was far from clear and I had, temporarily, double vision. But seeing two of everything didn't aid me to see even one way out. The airlock door now lay at the bottom of the slope. It was made of transparent clearplast, too. Through it I could see the upper portion of the half-buried diamond block, jammed tight behind it and making an effective door-stop.

I turned my regard to the crack in the slanting ceiling. It, at least, was within reach. I took the heftiest spanner in the tool chest and smashed away at the crack, trying to make it spread and widen. As I should have known from experience, I couldn't even chip the clearplast.

Presently, I stopped wasting my time that way and sat there wasting it in another: trying to think of some other way out.

'Hey, there. Remember me?' asked Lou. 'You haven't asked whether I'm still alive.'

'All right, are you still alive?'

I knew she was, and more alive than I was. The first thing I did after we'd stopped bouncing was to take a look at her. And note that her eyes were bright with excitement, that she was half smiling, and that – even though she was the quarry – she was enjoying the thrill of the chase and its climax. Maybe this love of adventure ran in the family: life was at its sweetest when the hunt was up, from whatever angle one viewed it.

I was no Marley, and would have preferred another angle to this one.

Pettigue, now, had viewed it from another angle: from the porthole of Lou's cabin, which happened to be on this side of the ship – I could see it from my tilted driving-seat.

'Thank God you *are* still alive,' he quavered. 'I saw the whole thing. I thought it was all up with me.'

'What makes you think it isn't?' I said, crossly, annoyed by his egocentricity. 'So far as I can see, we don't have a chance of getting out of here. The door's obviously jammed. The roof's cracked and we've lost our air. I've tried to break through it both with a spanner and my head, but it's tougher than either. Sorry, Pet, but there you are, that's how it is. It looks to be all up with us, and that means it's all up with you, too.'

That blunt summing up must have near paralysed him, for he could make no reply.

But Lou said: 'Oh, dear. Is it that bad, Franz?'

She wasn't smiling now, and I had the small melancholy satisfaction of realizing that I had sobered her.

'Let's see.' I edged awkwardly from my seat, slid down the sloping floor and hit the airlock door hard with my feet. It didn't budge a millimetre.

Silently and futilely I cursed the designers of the runabout. This particular door was the only one belonging to any airlock I'd seen which opened inwards, into the lock itself. They explained it had to be that way to allow for the positioning of the rear seats and also to avoid cutting into the storage space.

One couldn't blame them for not anticipating a situation like this. But, just because of that one peculiarity of design, we had to die and the *Endeavour* would never return to Earth – not from this expedition, anyhow.

However, it was my nature to kick against the pricks, so I began to take it out on that door, with my heavy boots. Lou slid down and joined me. We braced ourselves against one of the rear seats and shoved with our feet and all of our might. We might as well have tried to push a brick wall over.

Pettigue came through timidly: 'Any luck, Captain?'

I lay back, resting and taking stock, and didn't answer immediately.

High above, the remaining blocks were still circling, quite slowly now, against the stars. I doubted if they could muster a single conscious thought between them, but I found myself identifying them with tigers: so long as we stayed put, we were reasonably safe: it was movement which attracted their attention and invited them to pounce.

Which may or may not have been true. What was certainly true was that if we didn't move, we should die soon, anyhow, from gradual suffocation. There was only so much air in the cylinders of our space-suits: they were already more than half empty.

I said, irritably: 'What the hell has luck to do with it, Pettigue?'

Knowing well enough that it had everything to do with it. If that confounded Marlionum sheet hadn't stuck across the windscreen at just the wrong moment... If the runabout had been designed just a little differently... If I hadn't locked Pettigue in that cabin...

Lou said, gently: 'No, we can't get out, Mr Pettigue. So I'm afraid we'll have to ask you to come and rescue us.'

I snapped: 'Don't be so bloody silly, Lou. He can't get out either.'

She ignored that. 'Mr Pettigue, look under the mattress of my bunk. You'll find another key to the cabin.'

I stared at her in speechless surprise.

She smiled at me. 'I'll explain later, dear… Have you found it, Mr Pettigue?'

But Mr Pettigue's transmitter remained silent.

'Pet,' I called, impatiently, 'did you get that message?'

No answer.

I climbed back to my seat so that I could see the ship and particularly the porthole of Lou's former cabin. What else I expected to see, I couldn't formulate. But there was something else.

Another game of Ring-a-Ring-of-Roses was in progress. This time it was a score or so of thin Marlionum sheets, stiff as boards, sailing around the ship on a plane just above that cabin porthole. They reminded me of a stock scene in the old Western films: the Red Indians riding around, then closing in on the last few survivors in the besieged fort.

The big difference here was that the fort could take off and shoot away to safety, carrying its last survivor with it. It was strange how Pettigue always seemed to be cast for the rôle of the last survivor.

I stared gloomily at the merry-go-round and muttered: 'Well, that finally does it.'

The spare key didn't matter any more, not to us, anyhow. It would give Pettigue his freedom and probably his life, too. But it would do nothing for us.

Pettigue was scared to venture out on the moon even when there were no Indians around. His nerve had already broken once under the strain of being exposed to the vast reaches of emptiness. Since then – it had been obvious from his manner – he had been the shrinking prey of his fears, going rapidly to pieces.

He could never bring himself to set foot outside the ship again, let alone cross the two hundred metres of open ground, under the threat of an unpleasant death from the hovering diamonds, merely on the slim chance of being able to help us.

Not when he knew he had only to press a few buttons to lift himself right out of this mess.

'What finally does what?' asked Lou, having climbed up beside me.

Then she saw what I saw. Moreover, she saw something which I hadn't seen.

She whispered: 'Franz, look at that!'

I followed the indication of her forefinger.

The Marlionum sheet which had lodged against the radio aerial was still there, but it was no longer recognizable as a sheet. It had wound itself in tight, wire-like coils, criss-crossing around the aerial rod as though it were trying to choke it to death.

We both recognized the pattern. We had seen it before – on the water pump of Colonel Marley's space-suit.

'That was the way it happened, all right,' I said, slowly. 'You were quite right, Lou.'

She studied the effect for a while in silence, then said: 'Yes, and Mr Pettigue was right, too. Marlionum contains some form of organic life.'

If Pettigue heard that, he made no comment.

I looked at the *Endeavour* again, but the only signs of life and movement were those of the strange element itself, tirelessly sailing around and around.

I checked our air cylinders. The indicators registered even lower figures than I'd hoped. We had used up a lot of energy – and therefore oxygen – in attacking that door. I cursed myself for not storing some spare cylinders in the runabout, and then reflected that it wouldn't have changed the situation much if I had done so. The end would be the same, only more protracted.

I could summon no more hope. This was the moment of truth, the acceptance of the inevitable.

'Now, Pettigue,' I said, 'pull yourself together and listen to what I say. Never mind us: we've had it. We don't blame you: you can't help the way you're made. You're free to go. I taught you how to handle the ship. It's easy enough, but if you've forgotten any of it, ask me about it now, my time is limited. There's just one other thing – and make a note of it.'

I described the behaviour of Marlionum when crumpled around another metallic object, instancing the case of the aerial.

'This proves that Colonel Marley's death was purely accidental,' I went on, 'so don't let them fix the blame on you... *or on anyone else*. Sorry we couldn't get the new stock of Marlionum to you. We have it stashed in the back here: it seems inert and harmless enough. So it appears that only odd patches of the stuff, here and there, react to the electro-magnetic field. Why there's this discrimination, I can't figure. Maybe you'll work it out for yourself one day. Well, I guess that's all. Can you think of anything else, Lou?'

I paused.

'No,' she said. 'What more is there to say? Who's there back home to send last messages or love to? I've no relatives left now.

No friends… not even little Mack. The only person who matters to me is here with me.'

I had nothing to add, either, and for the same reasons. There wasn't another human being I cared about or who cared two cents about me. All my love was centred on Lou, and at this moment I felt pretty full of it.

'Pettigue, did you get that?' I inquired.

The silence itself said no.

I divined that I had only been wasting my breath, and breath was precious now. I was baffled by Pettigue's total lack of response. Had he already suffered a nervous collapse before Lou mentioned the key? Was he too darned ashamed to say anything? Had he switched off the radio, unable to take our plea for the help he couldn't give? Or was he dead – somehow? Or was it merely that his radio had broken down?

The last seemed unlikely: there were several transmitters in the ship.

However, we should never know now; the speculation was futile.

I embraced Lou, so far as it was possible: these damnable space-suits would keep us apart to the very end.

I didn't want her to dwell on that end, so I broached another subject.

'You said you would explain about that second key.'

'Oh, yes. It's a phobia or something. It dates back to my early fights with Dad. When I became really unruly, and sometimes violent, he would lock me in my bedroom until I cooled off. At first, he made the mistake of leaving the key in the lock. I would poke it out with a hairpin until it fell on to a sheet of newspaper that I'd pushed under the door.'

'That's an old trick, love.'

'Yes, and he soon tumbled to it. So, after that, he would always put the key in his pocket. But it didn't do any good. I'd had a replica made in the meantime and kept it hidden under my mattress. He never learned how I got out. He was always going to fix an outside bolt on the door, but never got around to it. Poor Dad. I suppose he meant well in his crazy way. I gave him hell sometimes – but, then, he gave it to me, too.'

'But, surely, you didn't really believe he might lock his grown-up daughter in her cabin on the *Endeavour*?'

'Grown-up? When was I ever grown-up, Franz? Yes, of course I believed he might do that. After all, it wasn't my idea to have my cabin fitted with a lock: it was his. So I took the usual precaution. Odd, I'd quite forgotten about the key – until a few minutes ago. Maybe because after Dad died I had no further need of it.'

She fell silent. Possibly she was reflecting that neither of us had any further need of anything in the material world. I wanted to assure her that it didn't matter. I wanted to tell her what she meant to me, but I couldn't find any phrases that didn't sound corny.

I expect she understood, anyhow.

Then the silence was broken in a sudden and unexpected way.

'Pettigue calling Captain Brunel and Miss Marley. I'm coming out to you now. Keep your fingers crossed.'

I could hardly believe my ears. I wanted him to say it again. Then I saw the secondary airlock door open on the side of the ship and a small space-suited figure emerge, feeling for the rungs of the ladder.

Lou and I stared at each other, confused with surprise, new hope, and a wonderful feeling of relief.

We sat up, tense, watching. Watching Pettigue, the circling sheets above him, the circling blocks above us.

I said: 'Thanks, Pet. We're watching and we're with you. Good luck.'

Spiritedly, he flung my own words back in my teeth.

'What the hell has luck to do with it?'

It was the voice of a man who had made up his mind at last and to hell with everything. I felt heartened.

He reached the ground. He came in shallow leaps towards us.

We divided our attention between him and the small cluster of diamond blocks still moving around the same spot in the sky. At any moment we expected one to dive at him and we were keyed up ready to warn him.

He was making good speed and we could hear his heavy breathing.

When he was about halfway to us I noticed the rock drill slung from his belt. I was still further encouraged. This new Pettigue knew what he was about.

He came on, and still none of the flying blocks deviated from its circular tour. Maybe they were alert for bigger game, such as another runabout. Or maybe they didn't detect him at all.

Anyhow, he arrived beside our wrecked vehicle, unharmed, unattacked, with sweat on his face and determination in his pale eyes. He gave us a sketchy wave as he paused to regain some breath. Then he pressed his drill against the curving clearplast roof and started it.

Under the merciless vibrations, the existing crack lengthened. Other cracks appeared and spread around it. Then, all at once, the whole top of the bubble broke into triangular fragments and fell away. It was like someone breaking open a hollow chocolate Easter egg.

Lou and I cheered. Pettigue grimaced in acknowledgement: something between a shy smile and a selfconscious smirk. We stood on our seats and scrambled out. I thumped Pettigue on the back.

'Great work, Pet – thanks. You showed 'em, all right.'

'I showed *me* – that's the main thing.'

I had never imagined the dry little fellow could look so happy.

We started out for the ship. I kept glancing, still apprehensively, at the blocks overhead. Even the three of us scuttling along far below didn't seem to interest them. Or maybe they were aware that the matter was already receiving attention…

Lou said, suddenly: 'Those sheets flying around the ship – there's only half of them left. Where have the others gone?'

I checked. She was right. The circle had thinned, appreciably. There were only nine or ten sheets left in the procession. We slowed to a cautious walk, gazing all around. But we couldn't spot the missing diamond shapes. That didn't mean, though, that they weren't somewhere nearby: they could be holding positions edge on to us and therefore be all but invisible.

'Start running again,' I said. 'Fast as you can.'

We resumed our dash to the ship. And, before our eyes, the remaining diamond sheets began to pass from sight, one by one.

But we saw how the trick was done, now. One diamond kept overtaking the one in front of it. It would slide alongside until it matched, and the two clung together, merged into one.

It was, of course, the same process which L. A. Marley and I had witnessed at the Tycho ray, only now it was happening in the vertical plane.

The constantly overtaking diamond was actually the sum of all those sheets which had seemed to have vanished. Steadily it became thicker as it travelled on. However, as there had been only twenty or so sheets originally, its eventual thickness couldn't exceed, say, a quarter of an inch.

All the same, a quarter-inch plate of that size, sharply pointed at either end, speeding through the vacuum, could be lethal. It might or might not smash a face-plate but there was no doubt it could rip holes in our space-suit material, tough and metallic though that was. Just one hole would be enough.

We were fifty metres from the ship when the thing completed itself and began spiralling upwards around the hull, past my little ball of a cabin, gaining height and speed simultaneously. Obviously, it was winding itself up for a power-dive.

I was sweat-soaked and out of breath. Running races in space-suits wasn't my idea of healthy exercise.

I gasped: 'Split up. Lou, you keep straight on. Pet, you veer left.'

I veered right. The idea was to scatter the target. Instead of the group, only one of us could be selected as the primary objective. I prayed it wouldn't be Lou.

We ran on in our different directions. The diamond ceased climbing, hovered, then seemed to be aiming itself.

It came down at the speed of a rocket.

I saw that it had picked Pettigue.

'Look out, Pet!' I yelled.

But he was doing just that. He flung himself sideways as the diamond went like an arrow for his chest. It drove into the bedrock not a metre from his feet.

He astounded me yet again. He scrambled up, unhooked his rock drill, and clapped it to one of the upper edges of the diamond. He worked his way along to the obtuse angle at the side.

'Leave it, man,' I called. 'That thing might pull itself free—'

Then I shut up. For the seemingly solid plate collapsed into a heap of loose diamond shapes as floppy as wet cardboard.

I heard Lou laughing. 'Why, you're nothing but a pack of cards!' she cried, like Alice in Wonderland.

Pettigue panted: 'Help me get these to the ship.'

I cocked an apprehensive eye at the real big fellows still lazily circling up there. They gave no indication of launching an attack. I had the feeling that, even if they did, Pettigue wouldn't abandon this gratuitous replenishment of his Marlionum stock.

Lou and I went over to him, grabbed some of the sheets and rolled them up like parchment.

Then we all dashed to the airlock ladder.

I made Lou climb first and Pettigue next – he was full of bravado now and wanted to be last, but I pulled my rank on him.

We bundled into the lock. The sight of the outer door closing to shut out the barren but perilous wastes of the Mare Nubium was gratifying.

While we waited for the air pressure to build, we talked.

I said thanks again to Pettigue, and asked if he had heard me tell him to abandon us.

'No. I didn't. I was pretty mixed up. Afraid, despairing, and yet angry. Lord, was I angry! I was sick and tired of being hounded by the same old spectre of disaster, the same old malignant fate. I wanted, like Beethoven, to turn on it and seize it by the throat. Yet at the same time I was scared, and wanted to run and hide from it. I could do neither. I couldn't move one way or the other. I thought I would explode from sheer impotence.'

'But you must have heard me tell you about the key,' said Lou.

'Yes, I heard that. It was the last thing I actually remember hearing. I rolled the mattress back and saw the key. It sort of hypnotized me. I just stood staring at it, blind to everything else. It seemed the ultimate symbol. It was the key to escape and safety – for I was fairly sure I could get the *Endeavour* back to Earth single-handed: the Captain's tuition had been thorough.'

'Thanks,' I murmured, modestly.

'Yes, it was the key to survival, but I had travelled that road before and it always led me to a living hell. Alternatively, it was the key to danger, possible death, but certain honour. "To pluck bright honour from the pale-faced moon…" I dithered between the two choices, as helpless as Balaam's ass. I nearly went crazy from indecision. I knew this was the crux of my life and yet I stood there like an idiot, utterly confused. Lord knows how long that state of conflict lasted. It seemed a lifetime in itself. Then, all of a sudden, the decision was made. Just like that. Not consciously at all: my subconscious decided for me. I knew exactly what I must do – there was no further question. And for the first time in my life I knew peace of soul.'

He gave a little sigh, and paused. We waited, unmindful of the pressure gauge.

He went on: 'I seized the key and let myself out. I hurried to the signals room and contacted G.H.Q. I told them the situation and what I proposed to do about it. I gave them the essential dope about Marlionum, just in case I never returned. At the same time, I was struggling to get my suit on. I was pretty busy. That's why I didn't get your calls. Sorry about that.'

'Sorry,' I repeated. 'He's sorry, Lou.'

'He's not sorry about a thing,' she smiled.

'You're perfectly right, Miss Marley. I chose right – at last. I feel good.'

I noticed that the airlock cycling was over – had probably been over for some time – and unfastened the inner door.

I left the other two discussing whether they should revert to their old cabins or not, and went to report to G.H.Q. that we were safe, thanks to Pettigue, and should be blasting off shortly. I added that we should be bringing samples of Marlionum.

That postscript, as it turned out, was unconsciously ironic.

The count-down checks were made without a hitch and the blast-off itself went just as smoothly.

The Mare Nubium began dropping away steadily. The ray of Tycho, which had played so much havoc with us, came into view and lengthened mightily before an ever receding horizon.

We looked down at it, glad to be finished with it.

But it was not finished with us.

From the radar screens, we discovered we had company. Three diamond blocks, of the thick kind, were trailing us at no great distance. Probably they were members of the happy circle who had kept us on tenterhooks down on the Mare.

Lou commented: 'They're seeing us off the premises.'

'Do the premises extend a hundred kilos into space? If you ask me, they're a long way from home,' I said.

'It's strange that such phenomena haven't been observed before,' said Pettigue, frowning. 'That electro-magnetic field is obviously very far from being only local…'

'But the moon has no measurable magnetic field,' I said. 'So where's their motive force originating from? We still haven't touched two miles a second – the moon's escape velocity, of course – yet, so it can't be mere inertia that's keeping them on our tail. In fact, they're *increasing* speed – we're accelerating and yet they're keeping up with us. How, for Pete's sake?'

'*Why* would be more to the point,' murmured Lou.

'They must be using the most powerful electro-magnetic field of all: the sun's,' said Pettigue.

'I think,' said Lou, following her own train of thought, 'that they deliberately held their fire while we were three small separate targets. They were waiting to get us all together where they wanted us – out in space, so that if they miss their aim they won't just smash into the ground but have the chance to sweep around for another shot. Also, I think if anything's to be smashed, they want it to be the *Endeavour*.'

'They did this, they want that,' I said. 'You're endowing them with minds of their own.'

'No, I'm not really, Franz. They're only bundles of primitive impulses, hardly more complicated than a photo-electric cell.'

'Well, look out,' I said, grimly, 'here come your photo-electric cells.'

It was a three-pronged attack from different directions. Those bundles of primitive impulses had worked out a pretty sound battle plan. Whichever way the *Endeavour* dodged, it couldn't help moving into the path of one of them. It was as if they assumed that the ship was able to manœuvre as flexibly as they could. In fact, of course, it was limited to the forward direction, with some slight latitude allowed by the firing of the small side-jets.

I gave the ship a spurt in the said forward direction of sufficient power to have us sagging at the knees.

This made two of the blocks miss. They passed just under our tail into the superheated efflux stream and were melted to mere blobs.

The third struck us below the belt – under the tubular ring – in the region of the atomic reactor. The small assailant packed a terrific punch: it was like a blow from the hammer of Thor. My muscles contracted in anticipation of the blow-up.

It didn't come.

I checked from the TV camera ports covering the exterior of the ship from various angles. Although the deflector reduced the need of shielding to a minimum, there was a lead layer of moderate thickness between us and the reactor as a precaution against the odd leak.

The diamond had wedged itself in this shielding. Which was a lucky break for us, for had it instead pierced the doughnut ring of the living quarters, or any similarly thin-walled spot the end of the *Endeavour* and its crew would now be history.

As it was, a fairly irresistible force had met a not so immovable object. It had shoved the whole ship sideways.

And it continued to shove.

I had a dizzy spell at the controls, not so much doing things as assessing what could and what couldn't be done. The forward thrust of the HAPU was being seriously affected by the surprisingly strong side thrust of the Marlionum block.

Striking balances between what the meter dials said and what my fingers on the controls told me, I drew a rough parallelogram of forces in my mind. I judged we were diverging between five and seven degrees from true course, a grave deviation on the Moon-Earth orbital path.

This could be corrected by the side-jets, but they had been designed to handle only the expected minor adjustments. Therefore, their cylinders weren't all that capacious. When they became exhausted, there would be nothing left to counteract the unceasing pressure of the Marlionum block.

Quite apart from that, a further complication was looming up. We were approaching escape velocity, and when we reached it the atomic drive would cut out. In normal circumstances, we should then coast smoothly along under our own inertia. But now, instead, we should be pushed around by the block. 'Pushed around' was certainly the right term: indeed, we should be pushed around and around and around – around our centre of gravity, endlessly revolving, tail over nose, as we hurtled on.

At the same time, the ship would also start spinning around its longitudinal axis to provide artificial gravity for us, as before.

As beautiful a complex of motions – or acrobatic gyrations – as it was possible for a space-ship to perform.

I called G.H.Q. and outlined the developing situation.

As I finished, the main drive ceased automatically and the *Endeavour* went into the complicated spin I had predicted.

'Here we go – it's all happening,' I told them. 'I'll be interested to see how your robot pilot gets us out of this one.'

There was panic back there. There was quite a bit inside me, too, though I tried not to show it.

Apparently, I succeeded, for Pettigue said with the ghost of a smile: 'I'm glad to see you're getting your own back on the boffins, Captain.'

And Lou said: 'That's it, Franz – make them grovel.'

Their faith in me was both touching and frightening.

The star field had spun past the portholes many times before G.H.Q. came up again: 'Sorry, but we hadn't bargained for a situation like this. There doesn't seem a thing we can do. Have you any suggestion?'

'Yes,' I said, sarcastically. 'Send for Dr Zignawitsch. He knows all the answers.'

G.H.Q. said awkwardly: 'We did contact him, as a matter of fact. This is one answer he doesn't know. So we'll have to leave it to you, Captain. Good luck.'

It must have shaken them somewhat to hear a chorus of three voices demanding: 'What the hell has luck to do with it?'

I flexed my hands, then applied them carefully to the controls.

I was about to try to learn how to become a real space-pilot.

XIII

THE PRIME MINISTER, IN PERSON, WAS GOING TO MAKE THE presentation.

All the top brass of the Space Service were there.

And Zignawitsch.

I guessed he was there only because it would look strange if he, father of the HAPU, were not. His absence might be construed as a snub to some important personages, and in Zignawitsch's philosophy one mustn't risk upsetting one's superiors.

Besides the boffins there was a heavy sprinkling of laymen: reporters, journalists, assorted politicians…

And the whole affair was being televised, so we were warned to be sparing, on this occasion, of technical jargon. We were to aim at 'popular' expositions.

Lou said her piece first. She kept duly to the popular level: there was only a hint of L. A. Marley. She used the opportunity to turn the limelight on her father: his love of adventure, his drive, his determination to penetrate the mystery of Tycho's rays, his ultimate success – and how he paid for it with his life.

She was planting the seeds of a legend.

I thought the limelight was rose-coloured, but that's how legends are made.

'About my husband, Captain Brunel,' she continued, 'I shall say nothing except that none of us would have returned safely had it not been for his extraordinary skill. He will be telling you about that part of it presently, and I know him well enough to assure

you that anything I could say in praise of his ability would only
be eclipsed by his own account of it.'

Said with a sidelong, disarming smile at me – but it was the old
Lou, all right, with the cat claws unable to resist a dig.

She introduced Pettigue as the next speaker; no claws for him,
only an approving purr.

Pettigue got a bit technical about organic molecules. He quoted
Schrödinger pointing out, decades ago, that atomically there was
very little difference between living matter and what is called non-
living matter. Just one instance: it had long been known that the
structural change affecting metal called 'fatigue' is basically the
same as that which affects animal muscle.

He mentioned the many laboratory experiments in which it had
been shown that organic molecules – the molecules of life – could
be produced not only by violent electrical discharges but also by the
action of X-rays, cosmic rays, ultra-violet light, or volcanic heat.

Thus, Marlionum, although unique, was explicable in general
terms. Science was right to be excited by it, but had no real cause
to be surprised about it.

He went on to describe the known properties of Marlionum.

Although much work had been done recently by the leading
laboratories on the samples we'd brought back (particularly the
massive sample stuck like a thorn in the side of the ship), at the
moment we could only theorize about the behaviour of the element at its place of origin on the moon.

'I was going to say "in its natural surroundings",' said Pettigue.
'But its natural surroundings are almost any place. That is to say, it
reacts to and is sustained by the electro-magnetic field of the sun,
which reaches to the far boundaries of the solar system. However,
let us concern ourselves with Tycho's rays.'

He described how the stuff had, in molten form, splashed out from the crater of Tycho and dried in diamond-shaped scales. How the scales could build themselves into blocks, though this effect seemed to depend on the terrain and occur only in rare spots where the conditions were favourable.

First, the ground – to which, naturally, the molten element had moulded itself – must be flat.

'*Flat,* I emphasize,' he said, 'not necessarily level. In fact, we believe that where the ground is level a diamond scale is unable to move. By "flat" I mean that the scale has hardened and set in a perfectly flat plane – no bumps, curvature, or wrinkles. Any imperfections impair its adjustment to the lines of the magnetic field – we don't yet fully understand why this should be.

'Again, there seems to be a necessary take-off angle to enable a diamond shape to get off the ground and climb the lattices of the magnetic field. It's a pretty small angle, but the ground must slope by just that much. This explains why the take-off areas are rare. For all we know, we may have stumbled on the only one, although I personally rather doubt that. This stricture doesn't affect the general use of Marlionum, however. We can melt and remould it in flat sheets of any size, and set those sheets at any angle we choose – Captain Brunel will enlarge on the special technique arising from that process.'

He said that while, once moving in the magnetic field, there was nothing to stop either the blocks or the single sheets from sailing out into space – to a certain defined limit – there was no record of their having done so prior to the instance when they followed the *Endeavour.*

'It would seem,' he explained, 'that they need the attraction, or stimulus, or whatever of some alien body, metallic or partly metallic, to cause them to wander any distance from the enormous metallic mass of their own ray, which is their parent body. As we know, the *Endeavour* and its crew were the first such alien bodies to come near them – for maybe a million years or more. I mentioned a certain defined limit to their sailing through space. This limit is the cone of the moon's shadow cast by the sun. For we've discovered that direct sunlight nullifies their reaction to the magnetic field. Again, we don't quite understand why... yet. But it is so. Earthlight isn't strong enough to affect them, though. And so, like bats, they fly in the twilight. But in daylight, under the sun's glare, they lie inert. This is why the phenomenon of their flight hasn't been observed before now: astronomers have concentrated on observing the *illuminated* phases of the moon.'

My turn came, eventually. I felt a little sick. Although I was eager to have my say, stage-fright made it an ordeal.

So I began by quoting someone wiser than myself: such an ally provides reassurance, especially when he's my old favourite (my copy of *Virginibus Puerisque* was as dog-eared as Marley's copy of *The Trail of '98*).

'As Robert Louis Stevenson said in *Aes Triplex:* "It is a well-known fact that an immense proportion of boat accidents would never happen if people held the sheet in their hands instead of making it fast."

'That is the theme of my discourse.

'We must prefer to navigate with our own hands rather than let ourselves be borne away by winds blowing we know not where. We must be masters of our fate, not driftwood.

'The winds, tides, and currents of space are no less real than those of the sea – or of fashion. Space isn't empty, you know, just because it looks to be so. It's alive with movement, seething with conflict, a vast complex of radiation, ionized particles, and magnetic forces which, among other things, determine the geophysical environment of Earth and its neighbouring planets.

'And there's one hell of a prevailing wind blowing through it – the solar wind. The hot gas of the sun streams steadily outward under the pressure of expansion at a speed of something like a thousand kilometres a second. This gas from the sun's corona is in a highly ionized condition, which means that every cloud or whorl of it carries its own magnetic field with it. All streams of electrons pushed out by expansion pressure, or cast forth by electrical storms, in the solar atmosphere carry such magnetic fields.

'By pure chance, I happened to find myself in a situation where it was not only possible, but necessary, to test the reactions of a large block of Marlionum to this sea of moving magnetic fields.'

I told the audience how I discovered that when the rotation of the *Endeavour* swung the embedded block around to the sunlit side of the ship, the block completely lost its thrust. But that thrust reasserted itself each time the block swung back into shadow. Therefore, simply by controlling the ship's rotation, I could switch the drive of Marlionum on or off, so to speak.

This, however, wasn't sufficient for full navigation. It was like being in a sea-going ship with an engine and screw but no rudder.

My further experimenting revealed that the direction of thrust of Marlionum depended on the angle at which it was presented to a magnetic field. With the aid of the side-jets, and after much trial and error, I gradually acquired the feel of the interaction between the block and the lines of force of an electro-magnetic field. I learned to steer. I could make the ship not only ride with the solar wind, but also tack against it.

'My wife has always accused me of mixing my metaphors,' I said, 'so forgive me if I say it was like learning to fly by the seat of your pants.'

A laugh here (and I'd worked for it) from the Prime Minister, a former air pilot.

I continued: 'So much modern flying is little different from a desk job or sitting in front of a computer. In this age a born pilot tends to suffer from acute frustration: he yearns to have the feel of the plane – in these.'

I held up both hands.

There were murmurs of agreement, and a sudden outbreak of applause led by the P.M.

I had them now, and the stage-fright left me.

I pulled out all the stops. I was aware of Lou and Pettigue beside me at the speakers' table, encouraging me, sometimes *sotto voce* and sometimes not so *sotto*. But my main attention was on a beak-nosed fellow, dark, thin, and very tall, conspicuous in the third row because of that unusual height.

Zignawitsch.

I was brandishing a threat over the head of his child, the HAPU, which once had threatened me.

Marlionum would prove to be the basis for entirely new techniques in both powering and navigating space-ships. It was as though the old wind-jammers were coming back in a super-efficient form which yet offered positions for helmsmen, navigators, and master mariners – craftsmen, not robots; responsible men, not serfs of the computer.

The HAPU was doomed to remain an only child. And the space-pilot would far outlive it.

I took sadistic pleasure in making sure that Zignawitsch understood this. He realized I was rubbing it in for his especial benefit, and tried his old trick of pretending that I wasn't there – not really. He looked at his lap, or at the neck of the man in front of him, or closed his eyes as though he were bored.

But both he and I knew that playing ostrich wasn't going to help him.

Something had gone awry in his world of full automation. A few wretched human beings had dared to put the robot firmly in its place.

Consequently, space-pilots had a future. I had a future.

And, thanks to Lou, it wouldn't be a lonely future, either.

The cover illustration is by Chesley Bonestell (1888–1986), considered by many to be the dean of science-fiction artists. His work has adorned not only such books as *The Conquest of Space* by Willy Ley (1949) and *Beyond Jupiter: The Worlds of Tomorrow* (1972) with Arthur C. Clarke, but was also central to the films *Destination Moon* (1950), *War of the Worlds* (1953) and *Conquest of Space* (1955). His artistic career extended for eighty years from 1905 till his death. He was awarded a Special Achievement Hugo in 1974 and has both an asteroid and a crater on Mars named after him.

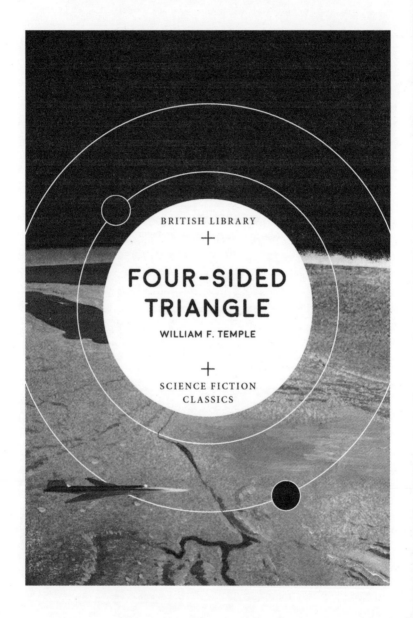

BRITISH LIBRARY

+

FOUR-SIDED TRIANGLE

WILLIAM F. TEMPLE

+

SCIENCE FICTION
CLASSICS